THE LAST WORD

"Here's to us, Shelby. To the two Lincoln-Douglas debaters. Dr. Lewis chose us to compete against each other." Matthew raised his ginger ale can to hers in a toast.

Shelby stared at him dumbfounded. It couldn't be possible that this was happening again. She tried to suppress the panic in her voice.

"I can't do the Lincoln-Douglas debate, Matthew. I can't." She looked up at him, but somehow it was Tom's face she saw, taut and angry, and she heard the echo of Tom's words—*a guy can't go out with a girl who upstages him all the time.*

"Are you afraid to lose, Shelby?" Matthew asked softly. "Are you afraid that might make a difference in the way you feel about me?"

Shelby was astonished. "Is that what you think? That I'm afraid to *lose*?" Shelby shook her head and looked up into his clear blue eyes. "The truth is, Matthew," she whispered, "I'm afraid to win."

Bantam Sweet Dreams Romances
Ask your bookseller for the books you have missed

The Last Word

Susan Blake

BANTAM BOOKS

TORONTO · NEW YORK · LONDON · SYDNEY · AUCKLAND

RL 6, IL age 11 and up

THE LAST WORD
A Bantam Book / April 1985

Cover photo by Pat Hill

ISBN 0-553-24718-2

Published simultaneously in the United States and Canada

*Bantam Books are published by Bantam Books, Inc. Its trademark,
consisting of the words ''Bantam Books'' and the portrayal of
a rooster, is Registered in U.S. Patent and Trademark Office
and in other countries. Marca Registrada. Bantam Books, Inc.,
666 Fifth Avenue, New York, New York 10103.*

PRINTED IN THE UNITED STATES OF AMERICA

O   0 9 8 7 6 5 4 3 2 1

The Last Word

Chapter One

If the invitation to the annual debate camp had come just a week earlier, Shelby would have been delirious with delight. Now, as she reread it slowly, every word echoed the emptiness she felt inside.

Dear Miss Scott:

Your high-school debate coach has enthusiastically recommended you for the annual debate camp at Northwestern State University. I am pleased to invite you to attend the month-long summer camp. The workshop will be attended by forty of the best debaters in the state. It will give you a challenging opportunity to polish your debate skills, while you make new friends. I hope you will accept our invitation. The enclosed brochure explains all the specifics of camp.

Shelby dropped the letter on her desk and reached over to pull the curtain on her window aside. Outside, it was raining with the violence of a late-May thunderstorm, causing her bedroom window to rattle noisily. The junior class picnic had been canceled by the rain just a few hours before, and everybody was disappointed. Except Shelby. She had felt an enormous sense of relief because she wouldn't have to endure the silent sympathy of her close friends or answer the questions of her other classmates, wondering why she wasn't with Tom. But most of all, she wouldn't have to bear the pain of seeing Tom with Holly.

Looking down at the letter, Shelby sighed. She would have been so happy about the invitation to attend the debate camp—if only it had come before her terrible argument with Tom.

For the hundredth time Shelby thought about what had happened three days before. No, she couldn't call it an argument, she reminded herself unhappily. Arguments had two sides, and this had only one side—Tom's. She had just listened, stunned into silence. For once she'd had nothing to say. There *wasn't* anything to say.

It had happened the previous Sunday when Tom had come over to watch television. Sunday evenings Tom and Shelby always spent together, watching their favorite shows, making popcorn, and wandering out into the backyard to watch the stars come out. That evening when Tom came into the den, Shelby was already watching TV. But instead of saying hello, he just stood, leaning against the door, watching her.

After a minute Shelby glanced up from the heap of pillows where she was snugly settled. She smiled welcomingly. Tom had been her boyfriend for years, but she always felt the same way when he came into a room. It was as though everything suddenly clicked back into focus. Her whole world felt right and comfortable again.

That night Tom didn't drop to the floor beside her as he usually did, but remained standing. "Let's go outside, Shel," he said quietly, glancing at Shelby's younger brother Roger. Long ago Tom had affectionately nicknamed Roger "Snoopy." "What else can we call him?" he complained. "He's always hanging around, listening to us." Now, Roger was draped across the sofa. He was wearing a pair of stereo earphones over his ears, and his eyes were glued to the television.

"But this show just came on," Shelby

objected, frowning. She patted the pillow next to her. "Come and sit down, Tom. We can talk here. Roger's tuned into the stereo—he'll never hear us."

Tom's gray eyes were clouded with a look Shelby couldn't read. She noticed that his blond hair was mussed, the way it got when he ran his fingers through it, a sure sign that he was worried about something. "I don't want to watch TV tonight, Shelby," he said abruptly, turning toward the french doors that opened onto the patio. "I want to talk."

"Oh, OK, if you insist." In general, Tom was pretty easygoing, and this mysterious behavior was very unusual. Curious, Shelby got to her feet and followed him outside.

On the patio Tom stood with his back to Shelby. His hands were shoved into the front pockets of his jeans, and he was looking up at the tall willow tree where they'd built a tree house nearly five years earlier, the summer before they both turned twelve. Tom had been in charge of cutting the lumber and nailing the frame together. Shelby had been the "ground support crew," as he'd called her, sending up tools, nails, and lumber in a complicated bucket-and-pulley contraption that Tom had invented. Shelby knew if she looked up, she'd see the gray, weathered planks of wood over her head. The tree house was still sturdy and strong. To her, it had always been a warm, loving reminder of the permanence of their relationship, a reminder that together they'd built something lasting.

But she wasn't looking up just then. She was watching Tom with growing apprehension as he stared into the shadows at the edge of the yard.

"Tom, is there something wrong?" she asked finally, a note of concern in her voice. "Why are you acting like this?"

"Shelby, there's something I've got to tell you." Tom wheeled around and faced her, his shoulders hunched crookedly in a gesture that Shelby had seen hundreds of times. It meant that he was about to say something he thought was very important. Somehow, the gesture touched her, and a sudden wave of affection washed through her.

"Well?" She looked at him expectantly, trying not to smile. When Tom was thinking, he pulled his eyebrows together and wrinkled his nose in a way that was almost comical. But that night there was a look in his eyes that was very serious. Shelby felt a sudden, inexplicable uneasiness. She wasn't sure what he was going to say—and that in itself was strange since she knew him better than anyone else in the whole world. After all, she and Tom had been in love—well, for always—since they were little kids. They'd lived on the same block, gone to the same schools, studied together, debated together on the school debate team. To Shelby, loving Tom was as natural as breathing. She couldn't remember when she hadn't, and she couldn't imagine when she wouldn't.

Shelby took a step forward and then stopped, waiting for Tom to say whatever he was going to say. When he cleared his throat and spoke at last, the words came with a shattering impact.

"Shelby, I think it's time we stopped seeing each other."

For a moment Shelby could only stare stupidly at him. Tom's words seemed to splinter the fragile evening silence like an explosion.

"Stop seeing each other?" she whispered at last, trying to find her voice. Her knees felt terribly wobbly, and she sank down on a lawn chair. "Tom, I—I can't believe—"

"I've been trying to tell you all spring," Tom went on flatly, as though she hadn't said anything. He wasn't looking at her. "I kept thinking you'd notice it, too, and maybe try to do something about it. But it just kept getting worse, and I can't go on like this any longer."

"Notice? Getting worse?" Her voice was coming back again shakily. She took a deep breath and tried to sound like her normal, everyday self. "Tom, I don't know what you're talking about. I haven't noticed anything different between us. Whatever's wrong, we can fix it if we try." In spite of her efforts, her voice broke raggedly. "Please, don't talk about something so awful as—as breaking up." Her heart seemed to be doing crazy flip-flops inside her chest. "I *need* you, Tom," she whispered, holding out her hand.

Tom half turned away, ignoring her hand. "You don't need me, Shelby. You don't need anybody. You can obviously take care of yourself."

Shelby shook her head, dazed. "I just don't understand what you're saying. Everything's been so good between us for such a long time."

"No, it hasn't, Shelby. It used to be, but things have changed. You've changed. When we were kids together, you were so sweet, kind of old-fashioned and shy and—soft." He looked up. "Remember when we built the tree house? We were a great team. We could work together without getting in each other's way. We didn't compete, we *helped* each other. You made me feel that I was really important in your life. That I really mattered." He sighed and scuffed at a stone with the toe of his canvas sneaker. Shelby started to say something, but Tom went on hurriedly.

"No, I've got to finish what I'm saying.

Things are different now, Shel. They started changing months ago, but you were so wrapped up in getting ready for the debate contest that you hardly noticed." He paused and thought, rubbing the back of his neck. "And the debate thing is making it worse. It's *making* you change. It seems like you always have to take charge of everything that's going on. And it's no fun even talking to you anymore—you always have to win the argument, no matter how it makes the other guy feel. You always have to have the last word." He turned and rocked back on his heels. His face was strained, and his lips trembled. "It's gotten so that winning means everything to you, Shelby," he said huskily. "It matters more to you than I do."

There it was. Shelby stared numbly at him, the terrible truth beginning to dawn on her. Winning arguments—taking charge. Tom had to be feeling this way because she'd won the debate in the school tournament, the most important debate event of the entire year. Most of the time debating was a team activity, and for the last couple of years she and Tom had debated together on a team. They had never been in direct competition. But this year was different. This year she and Tom had been in "pair debating." Instead of being part of a team, there had been just the two of them, arguing against each other. She'd won—and he'd lost.

Shelby swallowed hard. "Does this have anything to do with the debate?" she whispered.

Tom stepped back as if she had hit him, and his face was full of pain. "Well, what do you expect, Shel? A guy can't go out with a girl who upstages him all the time. It's nice for you that you won. You did a good job in the debate, really. You deserved to win, and I'm not jealous or anything like that. I can handle losing." He ran his fingers through his hair. "But I guess I can't handle losing to *you*. Losing the debate made me realize how I'd been feeling for the past six months—and why. I'm sorry. I guess being in debate for two years has changed you. And having both a mom and a dad who are lawyers is bound to make you more—more competitive. So, in a way, it's not your fault."

He looked at her, and Shelby could see in his eyes a trace of the way he used to feel about her. "I don't want to hurt you, Shelby," he said. His voice was low. "We've meant too much to each other. I still want us to be friends. But that's all. Just friends." He glanced up and, in an attempt at humor, added, "You can keep the house."

It was those words that crumbled Shelby's last resolve. She turned away, the tears burning her eyes. Tom watched her for a moment but made no move to touch her. Without another word he disappeared around the side of the house, leaving her standing there, tears running down her cheeks.

Now, although it was three whole days later, Shelby hadn't stopped thinking about that evening. She felt the salty tears gathering behind her lashes as she stared down at the letter. *What a cruel irony,* she thought. Every single person on the Hampton High debate squad, including Tom, would give anything for the chance to go to camp. Only one person from a school, the very best debater, was invited to spend a month on the college campus. Now she had the invitation—here it was, in black and white—and she didn't want it. Didn't want it because of all the things Tom had said. Didn't want it because being good at debate had meant losing Tom.

But the debate contest was only part of it, Tom had said. She propped her chin in her hands and stared dismally at the rain, thinking back over the past few months. Now she could remember little things that hadn't made much sense at the time.

There was the night at Barney's. The gang had been packed into the back booth, where they usually sat. She and Tom had been carrying on a silly mock-debate about some trivial question that Shelby didn't even care about. She had been enjoying the argument, enjoying testing herself against Tom. But all of a sudden it wasn't fun anymore because Tom just stopped talking. He hunched sullenly into the corner of the booth and began pleating his soda straw into a miniature accordian. He didn't say anything more all evening.

Then there was the snowy afternoon they were playing Scrabble on the floor in the den with Roger. Shelby had beaten them both by a couple hundred points. When she teased Tom about it, he had stalked into the kitchen to get another cup of hot chocolate. He spent the rest of the afternoon watching television and left early. His goodbye kiss was cool.

Even Roger, who was five years younger than Shelby, had noticed the way Tom acted. "Tom sure doesn't like to get beat," he'd observed the next morning at breakfast. "Especially when you rub it in."

Shelby had only laughed and helped herself to cereal. But her mother, who was on her way to the office, hadn't laughed. She had stopped putting papers into her briefcase and looked hard at her daughter. "Real winners don't make it tough on losers, Shelby," she observed dryly. "Someday you'll be on the losing side, and you'll be glad to have a gracious winner."

But Tom had said something else, something about "taking charge." She frowned. Most of the time he didn't seem to have any preference about what they did. So it was natural that she'd suggest something—a movie, maybe, or a drive to the lake or an evening roller-skating. He always seemed content to let her make plans for both of them. But now, with his words still in her ears, she could see that he must have resented her suggestions. Even if she hadn't meant to take charge, it had seemed that way to him.

Now that she thought about it, Shelby could remember a half-dozen similar events over the last year or so. They all added up to one devastating conclusion. She had lost Tom because she hadn't paid enough attention to his need to feel important. For him, the debate must have been the final, deciding factor in a long list of events that finally brought an end to their relationship.

Shelby thought back to the night of the debate. She could vividly recall the tension on Tom's face when he had stopped beside her on the stage of the school auditorium to wish her good luck. But she'd only nodded absently. She was concentrating on her notes, rehearsing her first arguments. Now, looking back, she could see that things might have turned out differently if she hadn't been so well prepared—and so anxious to win.

Shelby remembered how awful she had felt the first time she saw Tom and Holly together at Barney's, the day after the breakup. Holly looked even prettier than usual. She was sweet and petite and feminine, her long blond hair tied back with a pink ribbon into a ponytail that curled gracefully forward over her shoulder, her green eyes riveted on Tom's face. It was obvious that she knew how to make him feel masculine and important. From the look on his face, an unmistakable expression of pride and possessiveness that Shelby could read all the way across the room, it was clear that Holly made him feel like a winner.

Shelby looked out the window at the rain. Suddenly she knew what she had to do. If *winning* was her problem, going to debate camp and learning more about how to win would just make everything worse. Instead of going away to learn how to be more competitive, she ought to stay home and work on being *less* competitive, more like the girl Tom used to care about—or more like Holly.

Examining her face in the mirror that was propped up on the corner of her desk, she sighed. She wasn't exactly the feminine type, she thought. She certainly didn't have Holly's pretty, delicate, baby-doll features, and her straight brown hair was cut short like a boy's because it stubbornly insisted on frizzing in damp weather. She didn't have Holly's soft, feminine curves—she'd always liked sports, and her daily jogging had streamlined her.

With new determination, Shelby folded the letter and put it back in the envelope. The next day she would call her coach, thank him for the recommendation, and tell him that she wouldn't be going. Propping the envelope against the mirror, she thought about Tom and Holly, and the tears started again.

Chapter Two

The family was already at the table when Shelby came downstairs for dinner, red-eyed but composed. "Well," Mr. Scott said cheerfully as she took her usual place across from Roger, "I understand that something kind of nice happened to you today."

Shelby looked at her father blankly. Since the split with Tom, she couldn't think of *anything* nice that had happened. "Give me a clue," she said.

Her mother leaned forward, smiling. She still had on what Roger called her "lawyer suit," a gray, pinstriped skirt with a pink tailored blouse. It was a sure sign that Mrs. Scott had gotten home late from the office and they'd be having something very simple for dinner. "It begins with 'debate camp,' " she said, patting Shelby's hand. "Congratulations, Shelby."

"How did you know?" Shelby demanded angrily. She scowled at Roger, who was helping himself to a big spoonful of macaroni casserole. "That was my private mail. Nobody had a right to open it."

Shelby's father looked startled. "Nobody opened your mail," he said mildly. "I happened to run into your debate coach today. He told me you'd been accepted. He was very pleased."

Roger picked up an ear of corn and began to butter it messily. "What's the matter, Shel?" he asked. "Howie's cousin went last year, and he said it's a neat place. You get to live in the dorms just like the college kids. And there's this great lake smack in the middle of the campus, with canoes and ducks and everything." He pushed a shock of brown hair out of his eyes and left a smudge of butter across his nose. "If you're not going, maybe I can take your place," he added hopefully.

"Don't be silly, Roger," Mrs. Scott said calmly. She leaned over and used the corner of her napkin to wipe the butter off his face. "Of course Shelby's going."

Shelby played with the macaroni on her plate. She didn't look up. "As a matter of fact, I *have* decided not to go," she said. "There's a lot going on here in Hampton this summer, and I don't want to miss it."

Mr. Scott peered at her over his glasses. "Nonsense. What in the world could you find to do in Hampton that could be more important than debate camp?"

Roger winked broadly at Shelby. "Maybe something as important as getting Tom away from Holly? Is that it, huh?"

Pointedly, Shelby ignored Roger's teasing, but the damage had been done. Her mother glanced at her thoughtfully. "If getting together with Tom again is important to you, honey, the best way is to do *your* thing and let him do his. Chasing him or hanging around hoping he'll call isn't the way to do it."

Her father poured himself another glass of iced tea. "We're not going to tell you what to do," he said quietly. "You're old enough to make up your own mind. But you worked hard to earn the invitation, and one day you might look back and wish you'd taken it. And your mother's right." He gave his wife a half-smile. "You might get further with Tom if he had to wonder about all the guys you're meeting at camp. If you stay home, he can see what's going on in your life, and he won't have anything to wonder about."

"Yeah," Roger chimed in, "and think about all the fun you'll be missing if you don't go.

Howie's cousin says they went sailing and took hikes in the woods and did all kinds of great things. And at the end of the camp, there's this big debate tournament, and they give out trophies."

Shelby looked from one parent to the other and sighed. Why did her family always have to get into the act? "If I'm supposed to be so good at winning arguments," she said wryly, "how come I never win one at home?"

"This isn't an argument," her father said. "You're the one who has to make the decision. We're just offering advice. Now, who's ready for more macaroni?"

"It sounds like more than advice to me," Shelby muttered darkly. But deep down, she had to admit that what her parents were saying made sense. She knew she'd have a good time if she went. She thought about how much fun it would be to live in the dorm with the other kids, to have a roommate, somebody she could share everything with. And after dinner, as she sat in her room, she began to think that maybe her father was right about Tom. Maybe it would be better if he had to wonder what she was doing. Maybe he'd even begin to worry a little bit if he got a postcard from her describing the fun she was having and the new friends she'd made. After another hour of thinking, Shelby had made up her mind.

Shelby had never been away from home before, and after she had said her final good-bye to her parents and watched them drive away, she stood alone in the lounge of the college dorm at Northwestern State and felt a sharp stab of loneliness. But she didn't have time to think about it.

Just at that moment an older girl carrying a clipboard came barreling around the corner. She smiled when she saw Shelby. "Hi, I'm sorry I couldn't show you your room right away. Thanks for waiting, and welcome to Sanders Hall. I'm Wendy, your dorm monitor."

Shelby answered the smile tentatively. "I'm Shelby Scott."

Hurriedly Wendy consulted her clipboard. "Your room's on the second floor. Come on, I'll show you to it."

Together they carried Shelby's suitcases up a flight of stairs and down a long, carpeted hallway with doors along both sides. Some of the doors were open, and Shelby could see that a few girls had already moved in. Wendy pointed out the laundry room and the pink-tiled communal shower room, with a dozen showers and two bathtubs. Shelby was thinking of her private bathroom at home when Wendy glanced at her and began to laugh.

"It's OK, Shelby," she said over her shoulder as they continued down the hall. "You'll get used to the community showers. Everybody does—it's part of living in a dorm."

Shelby nodded uncertainly. Obviously, being the only girl in a small family had its advantages. She'd never had to share a room or a bathroom with anybody. This was going to be quite an experience.

At the end of the hall, Wendy unlocked a door. "Sorry I can't stay around and help you get settled, but I've got to check the other girls in." She handed Shelby the key. "Your roommate's name is Pamela. She'll be along pretty soon, and you can decide then who gets which bed and desk." Rushing off, Wendy ran down the hall, leaving Shelby alone in the room.

Shelby sat down on a bed, and the feeling of loneliness swept over her again. The drive to the college had taken only an hour. But in that hour she'd had enough time to feel separated from everything that was familiar and comfortable. Actually the feeling had begun the moment Tom had said goodbye. Her own room back in Hampton, so full of memories of him, was a hundred light-years away. There, in her own private place, everything had reminded her of the years of good times they'd shared together. Tom had helped her hang the cork bulletin board on her closet door. Even the poster collection that covered one wall was mostly made up of funny, sentimental gifts from Tom. There was the elephant poster that was meant to remind her of the time she forgot to make cookies for the fair; the huge lopsided, lipstick-red heart with "love" on it that had been the previous year's valentine from Tom; the autographed poster advertising the rock concert they went to on the night they'd started going together officially.

Shelby cleared her throat, trying to swallow the lump that had suddenly filled it. She didn't need posters to remind her of Tom—she would never forget him. Determined to make the best of things, she shook her head and looked around. Unlike her room at home, this one was empty and impersonal, brightened only by the yellow-plaid drapes that gave a soft yellow glow to the off-white walls. Two narrow beds were arranged side by side on one side of the room, with a desk between them, and two closets and two mirrored dressers were lined up along the other. There was another desk in front of the windows. Shelby went to the windows and pulled the drapes aside, letting in the afternoon sun.

The room itself might not be very special, she decided as she turned the crank that opened the old-fashioned casement windows, but it certainly had a special view. The college campus stretched along a tree-covered ridge, and just outside her window was a magnificent blue spruce that gave off a spicy, piney scent in the June sunshine. Through the branches she caught the silvery glimmer of the lake, pocketed in a soft green meadow and bordered by tall pine trees. Suddenly she felt better.

She turned back to the room with new determination, surveying it critically. It was kind of blank-looking, but it wouldn't be bad at all once she had personalized it a little bit. She was glad her mother had suggested bringing her yellow, quilted spread and yellow throw rug. With the drapes, the rug would add a sunny glow to the room. She pulled the spread out of her duffel bag and looked uncertainly at the two beds. The one nearest the window was obviously the better choice, she thought; if she slept there, she could hear the breeze in the tall spruce and awaken to the singing of birds in the morning. With sudden decisiveness, she got the blankets and sheets from the closet and began to make up the bed closest to the window.

When it was finished, Shelby felt better just looking at the familiar handmade spread. In another twenty minutes she had unpacked her suitcases and hung her clothes in one of the closets. There hadn't been enough hangers, but she had found more in the other closet. She set up her portable typewriter on the desk in front of the windows, and she'd just finished neatly stacking typing paper next to her file cards when she heard voices in the hall.

"I'm sure Shelby must be ready to get unpacked by now," Wendy was saying. "She got here almost an hour ago."

Wendy opened the door and stepped into the room. She was followed by a lithe, athletic-looking girl who was loaded down with suitcases, bags, and boxes. Her tawny hair hung in a single thick braid over her shoulder, but a mass of untidy curls had escaped from the braid and clustered damply on her neck. She was deeply tanned, and she carried a tennis racket under one arm.

"Shelby, this is Pamela," Wendy said. "Now that you're both here, you can decide how to organize the room."

Anxiously, Shelby turned to her new roommate. Would they be friends? "Hello, Pamela," she said tentatively.

"Everybody calls me Pam," the girl said, holding out her free hand. Her grip was strong and very firm, and her brown eyes were friendly. "Do you play tennis?" she asked.

Shelby shook her head, smiling. "Nope, sorry," she said apologetically. She'd signed up for lessons at the park the past summer, but Tom hadn't wanted to play, and somehow she'd never gotten around to going. Now she wished she had.

Wendy was looking at the made-up bed, frowning. "Shelby, I thought you were going to wait until Pam came before you decided how to divide up the room." She went to the closet and opened it. "Pam, it looks like you don't have any hangers. I thought we'd checked all these closets, but I guess we missed yours." There was a puzzled look on her face. "Sorry—maybe you and Shelby can share until we can find some for you."

Shelby blushed with embarrassment. "I guess the hangers are my fault. I was kind of anxious to get unpacked, and I just saw all those hangers in the closet and . . ." Her voice trailed away, and there was an awkward silence in the room.

"Well, I'm sure you'll get it straightened out," Wendy said crisply. "It might be a good idea to draw straws to see who gets the bed and the desk by the window."

"Oh, that's not necessary," Pam said. She went to the window to look out. "I probably won't be spending a lot of time here."

Shelby looked at Pam. Had she already

alienated her new roommate by being in such a hurry to get settled?

"It's not what's necessary, Pam, but what's fair." Wendy's voice was firm. "I'll leave you two to figure it out. Dinner is at six in the cafeteria on the other side of the lake. It's a red-brick building with the big glass windows." She went to the window to point. "If you follow that path, you'll come to a footbridge that'll take you across the lake. Don't forget to wear your plastic name tags—those are your meal tickets. If you forget your name tag, or if you're late, you'll miss dinner. And after dinner everybody meets in the assembly hall." She turned and looked at Shelby. "Next time, don't be in such a hurry to decide things," she said with an unmistakable note of disapproval in her voice. "A few more minutes of waiting wouldn't have hurt."

Shelby avoided looking at Pamela as Wendy went out of the room. A terrible awareness was growing on her. Tom had said she was always taking charge. And now she had gotten off on the wrong foot with both her dorm monitor *and* her new roommate—all in the same half hour. She cleared her throat, then said, "Look, I'm really sorry about the bed and the desk and the hangers. I—I was so anxious to get settled that I just didn't think."

"Don't worry about it, Shelby. Honestly. I'm perfectly satisfied just the way it is."

"But I *want* to be fair," Shelby insisted. She went to the desk and picked up a card. "Here, let's tear this into little pieces and draw for the biggest one."

But when they had drawn, Shelby saw to her embarrassment that she had won. "Let's draw again," she said, quickly scrambling the pieces.

"That's silly." Pam put her suitcase on the bed farthest from the window and unzipped it emphatically. She sounded impatient. "We've got more important things to do than worry about who gets the bed and the desk by the window. If we don't get moving, we'll be late for dinner. And that's where the fun begins—right?"

As she sat cross-legged on her bed and watched her new roommate unpack, Shelby couldn't figure out why she wished she had lost the draw.

Chapter Three

As Shelby trailed Pam down the path to the lake, she looked around eagerly. Roger's secondhand report had been accurate. The campus *was* beautiful. The paths were bordered by patches of wild flowers, and the meadow was lush and velvety and dotted with yellow daisies and blue cornflowers.

The lake lay at the bottom of the hill. Through the pine trees Shelby could see several red and yellow canoes, floating like bright autumn leaves along the shore, and a sailboat that seemed to skim across the surface. The water was crystal clear, reflecting the tall, billowy clouds and the sky.

"I wonder where they store the other sailboats," she said half to herself, thinking of Roger's suggestion. "It would be fun to go out on the lake and just drift with the current."

27

Suddenly Shelby was reminded of the summer before when she and Tom had spent dozens of marvelous afternoons playing in inner tubes at the lake just outside of Hampton. They had laughed and splashed each other, floating idly with the current, then madly racing each other to the shore. It seemed impossible that those wonderful times with Tom were gone. An aching hurt replaced the feeling of excited anticipation. Maybe she shouldn't have come, after all.

Pam had stopped in the middle of the path, and Shelby almost bumped into her. "I know where I'll be spending *my* free time," she said. She swung an imaginary tennis racket in the direction of the courts at the top of the hill and grinned wickedly. "I'm sure I can find some big, handsome guy with a ferocious backhand who is just as good on the tennis court as he is in debate. Look—the courts are even lighted so we can play at night!"

Shelby pushed the thought of Tom aside and smiled with an effort. "Maybe *you* can play at night," she said teasingly. "The rest of us will be spending our evenings in the library. Remember what the information sheet said? Six-thirty to nine-thirty every night."

"Oh, come on," Pam said, "there's bound to be *some* free time. They can't keep us cooped up all the time, can they? And, anyway, I simply *have* to make time for tennis. The week after camp is over, I'm playing in the city tournament back home, so I need to spend as much time as I can on the court. Even if that means skipping library."

Shelby looked at her curiously. "If tennis is so important, how come—"

"How come I'm here?" Pam hesitated. "Well, actually I'm not sure I ought to be. I'm the alternate. The girl who was first in our club couldn't come, so I'm here in her place. I don't think I'm a very good debater when you come right down to it," she confided. "But I thought it would be fun to come to camp." She looked at Shelby critically. "I'll bet you're a good debater, though," she added. "You look like a take-charge person."

Before Shelby could answer, Pam tugged at her arm. "Hey, look, there's the bridge Wendy was telling us about. Come on, I'll race you. Last one to the lake is flat-footed." With a lithe, athletic lope, Pam ran down the hill, her braid swinging.

Shelby followed her. Pam had called her a "take-charge person." She winced a little, remembering how she had taken charge of the room.

The wooden footbridge arched across the

lake at its narrowest point, and under it the water gurgled noisily as it ran over rocks.

Pam leaned over the wooden rail and dropped a twig into the water. "How romantic," she said dreamily. "I can't *wait* to see what the boys here are like, can you? I can just imagine standing here in the moonlight next to a tall, handsome boy who thinks I'm the greatest tennis player in the world."

Shelby frowned and threw a green leaf into the water. Why did everything have to remind her of Tom? "He probably wouldn't like you if you beat him," she replied shortly. The leaf spun dizzily into the middle of a tiny whirlpool and vanished. "Guys have trouble with girls who beat them."

Pam gave her a curious, sidelong glance. "Sounds like you're speaking from experience. Somebody you liked a lot?"

"Yes." Suddenly, for the first time since it happened, Shelby wanted to talk about it. "I've loved Tom since we were little kids. We grew up together. Then one night he just told me he didn't want to go out with me anymore." Pam's sympathetic silence encouraged her to go on, and the whole story came tumbling out in a rush of unhappy words.

"I really blew it," she finished sadly. "I thought arguing with Tom was just fun and games, the way it is in debate. Well, maybe it was fun for me. But not for him." She dropped another leaf into the whirlpool and watched it vanish. "It was all my fault."

"Maybe, maybe not," Pam said nonchalantly. "Maybe Tom just didn't like losing." She paused and laid her hand for a moment on Shelby's arm. "Listen, Shelby, don't let Tom ruin your time at camp. I know it's hard, but you have to try to forget about him and enjoy yourself." She glanced across the lake toward the cafeteria. "Hey, if we don't get moving, we're going to miss dinner. And I'm starving!" As they hurried toward the cafeteria, Shelby was silent. Pam was probably right—she had to stop thinking about Tom. But how could she forget him? It just wasn't possible.

In Hampton the school cafeteria was in a windowless brick building that the kids called the "Hampton High Jail." But at Northwestern State it was a huge room with a balcony and ceiling-high windows that looked out over the lake. And there was a larger assortment of food than Shelby had ever seen in any cafeteria.

"Isn't this terrific?" Pam asked enthusiastically as they carried their loaded trays into the noisy dining room. "I'll probably gain twenty pounds from all this food." She sighed as a tall, muscular boy in khaki shorts charged in front of them. "Wow, take a look at those shoulders," she whispered. "Let's follow him. He's headed toward three other guys sitting by the window."

Shelby hung back. "I don't know, Pam," she said doubtfully. "They look like they're having a private conversation."

Pam didn't hesitate. "Of course they are, silly," she said over her shoulder, heading toward their table. "But that's where the action is. Maybe one of them will want to play tennis tonight."

The boys at the table stopped talking when the girls came up. For a moment there was an uncomfortable pause, and then they stood and introduced themselves. Shelby found herself looking up at a tall, good-looking boy with straight black hair, dark-rimmed glasses, and the most improbable blue eyes she'd ever seen.

"Hi. I'm Matthew Benson," he said, pointing at his name tag and smiling.

Shelby set her tray down too hard and spilled her milk. She began mopping it up as she sat down. "I'm Shelby Scott." She fumbled desperately for something else to say, feeling the crimson flush creep along her cheeks. "Did—did you just get here?"

He sat down again at his place, directly across from her. "No, I came yesterday to help check the guys into their dorm," he said. And Shelby thought she could detect a note of arrogance in his voice. "I was here last year," he added in response to Shelby's curious expression. "So I know how things are arranged."

Shelby glanced at him with respect. Only the most promising debaters were invited back to camp for a second year, she knew. Matthew Benson must be one of the winners of last year's tournament. No wonder he seemed so—so sure of himself. She buttered her roll and took a bite. "Tell me what the camp's like," she asked hesitantly. "Is it true that they make us go to class from nine until three every day?"

Matthew threw her a sharp look, and Shelby felt herself blushing again. "Isn't that what you came for?" he demanded with barely disguised irritation. "If you came to camp looking for lots of free time to goof off, you're going to be disappointed. Sure, we have lots of fun. But we work hard—or at least, *some* of us work hard."

Shelby wished she could crawl under the table and hide. She really hadn't meant to sound as if she were trying to avoid hard work—she'd just been trying to make conversation. Numbly, she looked down at her plate. "Sorry," she muttered. "I didn't mean . . ." Her voice trailed off.

Matthew's mouth relaxed. "No, *I'm* sorry, Shelby," he said in a quieter tone. "I didn't mean to bite your head off. But you're the third person who's asked me how much work we have to do or how much time we have to spend in the library, and I guess it just got to me." His face softened. "Actually, there's time for tennis, if that's what you're into. Or you can swim or ride horses or hike or go sailing." He hesitated. "Of course, some squad leaders are tougher than others, and some of them give long library assignments to keep you in your room, even *after* the library closes." There was an amused glint in his blue eyes, and Shelby suddenly realized that she was staring at him. She turned away quickly and began eating her salad, hoping he hadn't noticed.

Just then a man with a straggly gray beard stood up on a chair, put two fingers in his mouth, and whistled shrilly for attention. He was wearing sneakers and a T-shirt with the words "Debaters Speak Up" across the front. Everybody stopped talking and looked up expectantly.

"Glad to see you all made it to dinner on time," the man said loudly over the clatter of dishes. "I hope everybody's settled in and unpacked because we've got a full evening's work ahead." There was a loud groan from several kids at the adjoining table, and everybody laughed. "I'll ignore that because I know how much all you competitive types have been looking forward to nonstop debating." Another ripple of laughter went through the room. "You've got ten minutes to finish eating and show up in the assembly hall so we can get down to business."

Shelby turned around to ask Matthew who the man was, but he had already pushed his chair back. "Nice to meet you, Shelby," he said abruptly. He was smiling slightly. "Hope I see you later." Shelby was surprised to find herself hoping that he meant what he said.

"Well, so much for tennis," Pam said regretfully as they settled into their third-row seats in the assembly hall and waited for things to get started. She brightened. "But I've found my first tennis partner. Did you notice? He's that gorgeous, blond muscle man I was talking to." She made a fist and flexed her forearm speculatively. "Wonder if there'll be time to play tomorrow?"

Shelby didn't have time to answer. A short, pleasant-looking young woman was standing on the stage, and everyone fell silent.

"Hello and welcome to State's annual debate camp," she said. "I'm Dr. Molly Lewis, director of debate here at the university. We're glad to see all of you, and I congratulate you on being selected to participate in the workshop this year. I know you'll have a good time—that's what you came for. But you're going to have to work, too, because we believe you're the best, and we want you to develop the talent in debate that each of you has already shown."

Pam snickered uneasily. "I feel like an imposter already," she whispered to Shelby.

"Tonight we're just going to cover the basics," Dr. Lewis continued. "I'll talk about the general schedule, class assignments, things to do for fun, and so on. The squad assistants are passing out information sheets. If you don't already have one, raise your hand."

As Shelby raised her hand, she saw Matthew standing at the end of her row, a thick sheaf of papers in his hand. Coolly, he nodded and passed a sheet in her direction. As she sat back in her seat and began to read, she wasn't the least bit surprised to learn that Matthew was a squad assistant.

The hour and a half of review and explanations went quickly. By the end of the period Shelby and Pam had a pretty good idea of what the next few weeks would be like. "Gosh, I knew it was going to be tough, but I didn't expect *this*," Pam whispered uneasily. She ran her finger down the class schedule. "Looks

like they've got us booked solid all day long."
She cocked her head and grinned. "But I'll bet
we can talk our squad leaders into letting us
off to take advantage of some of the terrific
scenery around here." She nodded in the
direction of a good-looking boy in cutoffs and
a ragged sweat shirt, and when he winked at
her, she smiled back confidently. Shelby
sighed. Pam made it look so easy.

When Dr. Lewis was finished, the man who
had interrupted dinner came up to the microphone. "I'm Mr. Kelly," he said, leaning casually against the podium. "But nobody bothers
with the mister part—I'm just plain Kelly to
you folks. While Dr. Lewis is in charge of the
intellectual life of this debate camp, I'm in
charge of fun and frivolity." There were scattered enthusiastic cheers from around the
hall, and Kelly raised his hand. "I hereby
declare that we've had enough intellectual life
for one evening. I propose that we adjourn to
the terrace by the lake, where we've got plenty
of snacks and soft drinks—enough to keep
you busy until curfew. Come on, everybody,
out to the terrace."

The twilight was cool and fragrant with the
rich smell of pine trees, and a slender crescent
moon was just rising over the lake by the time
Shelby and Pam elbowed their way to the
snack table on the terrace. Shelby had just

filled a plate with chips and dip when she looked up to see Matthew on the other side of the terrace. He was deep in conversation with Wendy, her dorm monitor. Wendy was looking directly at Shelby and shaking her head, and when she saw Shelby watching, she turned away quickly.

It was obvious that Wendy and Matthew were talking about her, and Shelby felt a sharp, painful stab as she remembered what had happened that afternoon. Wendy was undoubtedly telling Matthew what a stupid thing she'd done, organizing the room to suit herself before Pam got there. Suddenly the gaiety went out of the evening for Shelby. She turned to Pam and thrust her plate into her roommate's hands. "Here, you take this stuff. I'm going back to the dorm. It's been a long day, and I'm really worn out."

"But it's just a little after nine," Pam protested, trying to juggle both plates. "Come on, Shelby. Let's go talk to my new tennis partner. He's over there with that good-looking guy you were talking to in the cafeteria. And Wendy's over there, too."

Shelby shook her head violently. Matthew and Wendy were the *last* people she wanted to talk to just then. "I'm really tired. Don't wake me up when you come to bed."

The empty footbridge was painted silver by

the moonlight, and in the distance Shelby could hear the kids' laughter and see the lights of the terrace spilling onto the lake. She stood quietly for a few minutes, thinking about Tom. What was he doing right then, back in Hampton? Was he thinking about her? For a moment she could almost imagine him there next to her, his arm around her shoulders, his breath against her hair.

When she got back to the empty room, it was a long time before she fell asleep, and when she did, she dreamed of Tom and a golden summer afternoon.

Chapter Four

"I hope your morning was as terrific as mine was," Pam said breathlessly when she and Shelby met in the lunch line the next day. She hesitated between a bowl of raspberry Jell-O and a piece of chocolate cake with marshmallow frosting and then, with a gusty sigh, surrendered to the cake. "There's the most terrific-looking guy in my squad, and we're going to the library together tonight."

Shelby laughed a little enviously. Pam's relationships with people, especially with boys, were so easy and uncomplicated. "What happened to your tennis partner—the tall one with all the muscles?" she asked, reaching for a dish of vanilla pudding. "I thought you had a tennis date with him tonight."

Pam grinned, her brown eyes flashing.

"Actually, I've got two dates," she confided. "A tennis date before dinner, a library date after. What a life! At this rate, I might even learn to *like* debate."

Shelby moved over to make room by the desserts for one of the girls from her squad, a tall, pretty girl with almond-shaped, dark eyes. Her hair was pulled back with a bright green ribbon, and she wore a white blouse trimmed in the same green. Standing next to her, Shelby felt a little rumpled in her jeans and plaid blouse. "Laura, meet Pam, our star tennis player."

Pam grinned and held out her hand. "Hi, Laura. Do you—?" she began.

"Sure," Laura said. She sighed. "But I'm afraid I didn't bring my racket. I can only manage one thing at a time. And debate is enough for me right now."

Pam laughed as they started to look for seats in the crowded dining hall. "I guess I must really be obvious."

Laura pulled out a chair as they found three empty places at a noisy table. She raised her voice to be heard over the din. "Well, I wouldn't exactly say that. But if you're the girl I saw out on the court this morning before breakfast, you're way out of my league. I'd just be a drag for you." She made a wry face. "And, anyway,

41

Shelby and I have a real tyrant for a squad leader. I don't think this one is going to give us any time off for tennis—or breakfast, lunch, or dinner, for that matter," she added. "Right, Shelby?"

"Afraid so," Shelby said, sitting down. She caught herself looking around for Matthew and pulled her attention back sharply, just in time to pass Pam the salt.

Pam shook her head. "That bad, huh?" she asked sympathetically. "What's his name?"

Shelby glanced hesitantly at Laura, who was putting catsup on her hamburger. "It's not a him, it's a her named Donna," she said. "And I guess she's good. Anyway, she sure is tough. The kids say she's got a lot of experience and that her squads do well in the tournament. But she's a little—" She stopped. It wasn't fair to say that her new squad leader was impatient, but . . . She began again. "Let's just say that Donna doesn't like to be interrupted with questions that she thinks we're supposed to know the answers to. I don't think I made a very good first impression."

Boy, she thought to herself as she picked up her fork and started on her salad, *that has to be the understatement of the year*.

That morning, right after breakfast, Dr.

Lewis had met with everybody in the assembly hall to introduce the squad leaders. There were five of them, three boys and two girls, all college students. They all wore intent, serious looks. "Your squad leaders have been chosen because they enjoy working with debaters," Dr. Lewis said. "But they were also chosen because they have high expectations for their squads. We want you to look back on this experience as one of the toughest—but most rewarding—of your life."

Dr. Lewis also introduced the squad assistants, all of whom were second year debaters. They were wearing the same bright red T-shirts that Kelly had worn the night before, but with white shorts.

"The squad assistants will help the squad leaders organize your work sessions, and they'll be in the library every night to help you with your research," Dr. Lewis explained as she introduced them. "And in the last week of camp, they'll participate with the rest of you in the debate tournament." Matthew was introduced with the other squad assistants. When he stood up, Shelby flushed. From her questions the night before at supper, he must think that she was a lazy goof-off. And from what Wendy had told him, he probably thought she was selfish as well. Shelby was grateful that she was sitting so far back in the room that he couldn't read her face. With an effort, she focused her attention on Dr. Lewis, who was saying, "At the end of the first two weeks, after we get back from our Fourth-of-July break, you'll be assigned to a different group, so you'll have a chance to work with other people."

After the introductions, Dr. Lewis passed around sheets of paper announcing the squad assignments. While Dr. Lewis talked about the organization of the groups, Shelby anxiously scanned the page until she found her name. She was assigned to the C squad, under the direction of a girl named Donna. Shelby craned her neck curiously to catch a glimpse of her new squad leader, who was sitting at the front of the room. Donna was frowning as she turned to whisper something to the girl next to her. Her features were sharp and angular, and her red hair was pulled back into a ponytail. She looked like she really meant business. Shelby sighed. "Challenging," Dr. Lewis had said. Donna looked as though she thrived on challenges. And to make matters even worse, as Shelby turned back to the list she saw that Matthew's name was there, too. He was the assistant squad leader for her group!

During the second period, Shelby's squad

met in an upstairs conference room with a window that looked out toward the lake. Several cluttered bookshelves ran along one wall of the long, narrow room, and a blackboard was hung on the other. As Shelby took a seat at the table, she noticed that Matthew was sitting beside Donna, calmly surveying the room. Shelby frowned. He was wearing the same look of arrogance she thought she had seen on his face the day before.

"This is our squad room," Donna announced after the eight debaters and she had all settled around the long wooden table that occupied the center of the room. "You can keep your supplies here—your notebooks and file-card boxes—if you want to, instead of carrying them back and forth to your rooms. For the first half of the workshop, we'll meet here every afternoon to plan strategy and hold practice sessions. Then we can—"

Without thinking, Shelby blurted out, "What happens after the first half?"

Donna looked annoyed. She obviously didn't like being interrupted. "Everyone gets a new assignment after the Fourth-of-July break—remember?" she said curtly. "Dr. Lewis explained this morning that the first term continues until the Fourth-of-July weekend. After that, everybody goes home for a couple of days. When you come back, you'll be assigned to a different squad." She looked around the table sternly. Her green eyes were cool, and her voice was icily controlled. "OK, group, the first lesson that every debater needs to learn is how to listen. If you don't listen, you're going to miss something important—something that might help you to win a debate. Understand?" In the dead silence, the boy next to Shelby cleared his throat.

Embarrassed, Shelby sank back into her seat. Donna might have been talking to everyone, but Shelby knew that the squad leader's words were aimed directly at her. Yes, she remembered hearing about the new assignments. She *also* remembered her resolve not to jump into anything without thinking first. But why couldn't she remember it at the moment she was opening her big mouth? She'd behaved like a dummy. And worse yet, she'd done it in front of Matthew—again. Taking a deep breath, Shelby tried to concentrate on what was happening around her, but the room seemed charged with the echo of Donna's words, and she had trouble listening to what the others were saying.

No one else seemed to notice Shelby's embarrassment. At Donna's suggestion, the other members of the group had started introducing themselves and telling about their experiences in debate. Matthew started them off.

"I'm Matthew Benson," he said, and Shelby noticed how deep his voice was. "This is my second summer at camp. In real life I go to Hazelwood High, which is kind of like going to a one-room schoolhouse." Chuckles rippled around the room as Shelby recognized the name of a tiny town about fifty miles from Hampton. "No fooling," Matthew said. "There are only a couple hundred kids in the whole school, hardly enough to field a respectable football team." He grinned proudly and held up one finger. "We may be small, but we're good. Last spring we took first in advanced debate at State."

"That's right," Donna added, with what actually looked to Shelby like a smile. "Matthew's school has the best debate program in that region—they've been state champs for a couple of years." She turned to the blond, sunburned boy who was beside Matthew. "Next."

"I'm Pete Harkins," the boy said. His wide grin showed a gap between his front teeth. "My team only competed in novice class this year, but I'm ready for anything now." He turned to Shelby and glanced down at her white polo shirt, which had a Hampton High emblem on the pocket. "Don't tell me, let me guess." He scratched his head and wrinkled his forehead, pretending to think hard. "Hampton High, right?"

In the general laughter, Shelby introduced herself. "I was in pair debating this spring at Hampton," she added, remembering that they were supposed to say something about their debate experience.

Matthew leaned around Pete and stared at her. "Oh, yeah? How'd you do?" He sounded almost incredulous, Shelby thought.

"I won," she said hotly, the anger rising instantly inside her. What right did Matthew have to sound so—so unbelieving? He wasn't the only one who had ever won a debate.

Pete gave her a lazy smile. "Hey, I'm impressed," he drawled. "I've never done pair debating, but I understand it's harder because you don't have a teammate to back you up when you make a mistake. Right?"

Shelby was about to answer when Donna cut in sharply. "You can talk to Shelby about that later, Pete, on your own time. Let's get on with the introductions. We've got a lot of stuff to cover this morning."

"Yeah, Pete," one of the other guys added loudly. "Make time with Shelby on your own time."

Pete sat back with a sidelong grin and a wink at Shelby, who smiled back, grateful for his friendliness in what was beginning to feel like a very hostile group. For some reason, Donna seemed to be singling her out for disapproval, and she felt uncomfortable.

Of the remaining five squad members, three were girls, and Shelby listened carefully as they introduced themselves. One was Laura. "My teacher wanted me to get into debate because I was so shy," she explained easily, smiling around the table. "I could hardly say two words in front of strangers. But after a couple of months with the team, everything changed. Now my friends tease me about wanting to take over our school." She added confidently, "I just tell them I'm waiting until I'm elected student council president next fall—*then* I'll take over. After all, that's what student council presidents are supposed to do. Right?"

As everyone laughed, Shelby watched Laura, admiring the deft way she made a joke out of her obvious competitiveness. Sighing, Shelby wished she could develop such a lighthearted attitude to *her* problem.

After the introductions, Donna rapidly reviewed the week's schedule. "This week we'll be spending a lot of time on research, getting the evidence together and organizing our arguments. Each of you is responsible for collecting twenty pieces of evidence every night—what we call evidence cards. Next week we'll break up into two-person teams for a couple of practice rounds. Then, when the new assignments come out after the midsession break, you'll start getting ready for the tournament. Every team will present its case in the first elimination round, and successful teams will go on to later rounds."

She looked down at her notes to be sure she hadn't forgotten anything. "And, of course, the tournament also includes pair debating, which has become a star attraction around here. At the beginning of the fourth week, Dr. Lewis will select two debaters to go up against each other." She glanced around the room, her gaze flicking past Shelby. "Maybe one of you will be selected for pair debating, if you're good enough."

Shelby had been scribbling notes while the squad leader talked, but when Donna mentioned the pair debating, Shelby pushed down so hard on her pencil that the lead snapped. Pete handed her a pencil, and Shelby took it gratefully.

At the end of the morning session, Donna led the squad across the campus mall to the library. "You'll be spending a lot of time here," she cautioned as she showed them where the *Readers' Guide* was shelved. "So you'd better learn to use all the indexes and the card catalog."

Pete, who was standing next to Shelby, brushed his shoulder against hers and said in a loud stage whisper, "In other words, my children, don't waste any precious time passing love notes or watching the clock."

Donna frowned at him and went on talking as though she hadn't heard anything. "You'll be here in the evening collecting evidence. Matthew will be around to help out."

One of the other boys raised his hand tentatively. "Are we supposed to share all our evidence cards?" he asked. "I mean, my debate coach last year let us keep back a couple of pieces of evidence so we could have an edge over—"

Donna shook her head. "Nope. In this squad, everybody shares. The competitive difference isn't in what you know, it's the way you put your information to work. When you look at it that way, debate is like every other team sport. Each team member shares the job of gathering information." She paused as if to be sure that her words sank in.

"And another thing. Some debaters seem to want to get their work finished in a big hurry. And sometimes these people think it's OK to make up the evidence they need. We call it fabricating evidence—'fabbing,' for short." She paused again, and several people shifted uncomfortably. "Fabbing evidence is the worst thing a debater can do, in my opinion. It's a lot worse than doing poor work or missing deadlines. And if I find out that any of you have fabbed your evidence—and I'm a pretty good detective where that's concerned—I'll see that you're sent home. Got it?" Everybody in the group nodded uneasily, and they were unusually quiet as they broke up for lunch.

On the way to the cafeteria, Laura fell into step beside Shelby. "Whew, Donna's going to be tough, isn't she?"

"Yeah, she really seems to insist on rules," Shelby replied, thinking unhappily about the way the squad leader seemed to have singled her out. "Looks like we'll be spending a lot of our free time in the library, doesn't it?"

Laura laughed sarcastically. "Free time? *What* free time? She's got every single hour scheduled for the next two weeks." She paused, reflecting. "But by the time the tournament comes, I'll bet we'll be glad for the discipline. Somebody told me that Donna was a squad assistant for a couple of years before she became a squad leader and her kids have always done well in the tournament." She glanced reassuringly at Shelby. "Don't let her get you down, Shelby. A lot of us didn't catch that part about the first half arrangement— you weren't the only one. I think she was just trying to make a point about listening."

"I suppose so." Shelby nodded glumly. "But I wish she hadn't made her point at *my* expense."

Now, as the three of them were finishing their lunches, Shelby only half listened while Pam described the members of her squad and the boys she had met already.

"Actually," Laura added, "the best-looking boy on our squad is Matthew. He's our assistant squad leader." She fluttered her eyelashes demurely. "Tall, dark, and handsome in a remote kind of way." She giggled. "But he did seem sort of interested in Shelby."

Shelby came back to reality with a start. "Interested in *me*?" she said. Her voice squeaked, and she lowered it, embarrassed. "All that Mr. Matthew Benson is interested in, if you ask me, is *himself*."

Laura laughed. "Isn't that true about half the guys we know?" she asked. "Honestly, now."

"Well, maybe," Pam said, gulping her milk and pushing her chair back. "But after an hour on the tennis court, things sort of get evened out."

Laura shrugged. "See there, Shelby? All you have to do is beat Matthew Benson at his own game, whatever that is. Then he won't be so stuck on himself."

Shelby stood up. "Sure," she said dryly. "Sure thing. He's just one of the best debaters in the state, that's all. Beating him at his own game ought to be easy."

Chapter Five

That evening the library was full of debaters huddled together in little groups to work on their assignments. Shelby's squad had a long assignment from Donna, and her group gathered to work together in one of the large, brightly lit study areas. Matthew was already there, waiting for them.

"OK, gang, here's where we're going to make it or break it," he announced cheerfully as they all settled down. Laura and Shelby were sitting together, and Pete had found a seat next to them and was leaning back in his chair, his feet propped on the table. "Donna wants everybody to turn in twenty evidence cards tomorrow morning. Right?"

Pete groaned dramatically and pounded his forehead with the heel of his hand. "Can't you do something about that woman, Matt? She's a slave driver—even worse than my debate coach back home."

Matthew grinned sympathetically, and Shelby noticed that that night he seemed more friendly and approachable. "I know how you feel, but it's not all that tough, Pete. There's a lot to do, but we'll work together, and it won't seem like such a big job. OK, everybody ready to pitch in?" He looked around, and to Shelby's surprise she thought she saw him smile when he glanced at her.

"We'll start with a list of books and magazines. You'll go through them looking for information. When you find something, write it down." He held up his hand. "One important thing. Be really careful to include the source of your information—the name of your magazine or book—so you can find it again if you need to. At the end of the evening, I'll check your cards to see how you're coming along. Tomorrow we'll duplicate all the cards and file them in the boxes in the squad room."

Matthew paused and glanced quickly from Pete to Shelby, almost as if he were deciding something. "Shelby, you and Laura can start checking out the books on this list." He handed her a typed list of books and then turned back to Pete. "Pete, you and Joe can get started collecting these magazines." He raised his voice to speak to everyone. "Remember that we're especially interested in *current* information. Ten-year-old facts won't do us a heck of a lot of good in an argument."

As Laura and Shelby started for the stairs with their list of books, Pete touched Shelby's elbow and smiled. "Next time we'll let Matthew know that we want to work together. OK?" he whispered. "I have the distinct feeling that he doesn't want to assign us to the same job."

Shelby laughed self-consciously, wondering what she should say. For a second she wished she had had a little more experience with boys.

The squad members spent several hours reviewing the books and magazines and making notes on their evidence cards. Shelby and Laura worked well together, and by nine-thirty, when the lights blinked to signal that the library was closing, their cards were ready for Matthew to check. He looked them over carefully. Then, before he gave Shelby's back, he studied her for a long moment. Embarrassed, Shelby lowered her eyes to the stack of books she was carrying.

"You've done a pretty good job selecting evidence, Shelby," he said at last. "I think we'll be able to use everything you've collected." He hesitated. "How long have you been debating?"

"About two years," Shelby replied. She

shifted the books in her arms. For some reason she couldn't understand, talking to Matthew was difficult. It was probably his arrogant attitude.

Matthew took off his glasses and polished them on the front of his shirt. "What do you think of the camp so far?" he asked abruptly. Without his glasses, he looked much less intimidating.

Shelby swallowed. "Well, I guess it's too soon to tell." She thought of Donna and Wendy and the mistakes she had made already—and Matthew knew about every one of them. "I—I guess I've got a lot to learn," she said, trying to smile.

Matthew put his glasses back on. "You, me, everyone else. That's what we're here for." He paused a moment as though he wanted to say something else. "I worked with Donna last year," he said finally. "She's a first-rate coach. She's demanding, and she has high standards. But sometimes she seems—well, people who don't know her very well think she's kind of hard to get along with." He grinned, and the smile seemed to lighten his eyes. "Actually, Donna's easy to work with once you get to know her. And because she's tough, you'll learn a lot from her."

He handed Shelby's cards back to her, and their fingers touched. Her heart began to pound wildly, and she nodded, flustered, snatching her hand back as if she'd been burned. "OK, I'll try to remember that," she managed to say.

Walking back to the dorm with Laura through the warm June evening, Shelby thought of Tom. Matthew didn't have Tom's smooth, blond good looks, but there was something else about him, something honest and serious and—well, mature. At first she had thought that he was arrogant. But now it seemed less like arrogance and more like self-confidence. Considering the performance of his high-school debate team, Matthew obviously had something to be proud of. But then she thought of Tom again, and the easy, comfortable relationship they'd had until just a few weeks ago. When she was with Tom, she'd never felt awkward and uncomfortable, the way she had just then. Suddenly she felt terribly mixed-up and uncertain. Had she been right to come to camp? Would it have been better to have stayed home where she could see Tom? If she'd stayed home, would they be together right now?

During the rest of the week, Shelby asked herself that question a dozen times. Maybe she wouldn't have felt so unhappy if things had been going better in her squad meetings, she told herself. But as it was—well, *nothing* seemed to work out. Assembling evidence for the next week's practice debate was interesting and challenging, but after making a fool of herself that first day, Shelby couldn't seem to do anything right.

The next day she dropped a box of several hundred evidence cards all over the floor, and she could feel Donna's disapproving eyes on her while she hurriedly picked them up and sorted them into the right order. That afternoon she'd been talking to Laura at the beginning of the session and didn't notice that the meeting had begun until Donna said icily, "Shelby, if you and Laura will finish your conversation, we can get started."

And the next morning Shelby had left her assignment in her room and had had to go back for it, which made her nearly ten minutes late. Donna didn't actually say anything, but her disgusted expression spoke plainly: "Well, what can you expect from somebody as disorganized as Shelby."

As they left the squad room for lunch, Pete hurried to catch up with her. "You really looked down this morning, Shelby," he said. "Anything I can do?"

Shelby shook her head glumly. "I wish you could," she said. "But I'm afraid it's just *me*. I can't seem to do anything right where Donna's concerned."

Pete nodded with a knowing look. "Well, all of us have our problems with her if that's any consolation. Did you see the number of cards she assigned for tomorrow? First it was twenty a night—now thirty! The other squad leaders are only assigning half that many. With all the great things to do around here, it's criminal to make us stay in the library so late." He draped his arm across her shoulders and spoke into her ear. "Listen, Shelby, Kelly's organized a bowling tournament at the Student Union tonight after the library closes. How about it? We could even skip out of the library an hour early. Matthew probably won't even notice."

"Well . . ." Shelby hesitated. She had promised herself that she'd review all the evidence cards she had collected so far and organize them for next week's practice debate. And it really wasn't fair to Matthew to put him on the spot by sneaking out of the library.

"Oh, come on, Shel," Pete said. "You've been doing nothing but work ever since you got here. You deserve to have some *fun*." He grinned. "Everybody else is having fun—why not you?"

Pete was right about that, Shelby had to admit, suddenly feeling sorry for herself. Why *shouldn't* she go out with Pete? Summoning a smile, she nodded. "OK. But I really don't think we ought to leave an hour early. I'll never get tomorrow's assignment done."

"Well, half an hour, then," Pete conceded. "All you have to do is meet me behind the card catalog on the first floor. Matthew won't even miss us."

But it hadn't been as easy as that, of course. At eight-thirty, Shelby had met Pete, and they walked to the bowling alley in the basement of the Student Union. But as they were standing in line for their bowling balls, Donna suddenly materialized beside them. Shelby's heart turned over, and she thought guiltily of her unfinished assignment.

"I suppose both of you are ready for tomorrow," Donna said, glancing down at her watch. "That's why you left the library so early. Right?"

Pete shot Shelby a cautioning look and shook his head slightly. "All finished," he said cheerfully to Donna with an ingratiating smile. "Are you entering the bowling tournament, too?"

Donna shook her head. "Not tonight," she replied. "Too much work to do." She glanced meaningfully at Shelby. "I'll look forward to seeing your assignment tomorrow, Shelby."

"Worse luck," Pete said, letting his breath

out in a loud sigh. "Now she'll nag us the rest of the week.'" He paused, then grinned and reached for Shelby's hand. "But she's not going to keep us from winning that tournament tonight. Right, Shel?"

Meeting Donna had driven all the fun out of the evening for Shelby, but she didn't want Pete to know. "Sure," she said with as much enthusiasm as she could muster. And when Pete looked at her, she managed a smile. With an effort, she continued smiling for the next hour.

The next morning Donna called on Shelby first to review the assignment. Shelby had stayed up late to finish it, long after Pam had gone to bed. But she knew it wasn't a very good job, and she cringed when Donna said, "That's about what I expected."

As Shelby handed in her work, Matthew smiled at her. "It wasn't *that* bad, Shelby," he said in a low voice. "In fact, it was pretty good." She smiled back gratefully. Maybe if she just kept on trying, things would get better.

But that wasn't the way it turned out. In the squad meetings the rest of the week, Donna pointedly ignored Shelby's efforts. No matter how good Shelby thought her work was, Donna didn't seem to notice it. And to make matters worse, the other kids on the squad began to sense Shelby's frustration. Most of them—except for Laura and Pete, whose persistence was often as annoying as it was flattering—responded by leaving her alone.

Shelby's feelings of isolation spilled over into her other relationships. Laura was a good study partner, but she was dating a boy in another group, and the two of them spent their free time together. When Shelby was with them, she felt like an outsider.

Pam had found a whole string of new friends—most of them boys—and she rarely spent much time in the dorm room. Instead, she rushed in breathlessly at the last possible second before curfew or dropped in hurriedly to take a shower a few minutes before dinner. Shelby figured that Pam's squad leader must be a lot less demanding than Donna because Pam had hours of free time for tennis—with time left for swimming and horseback riding. At least a half-dozen guys apparently shared her sports interests because whenever Shelby ran into her roommate, Pam was with somebody different.

In a way, though, having Pam away so much of the time was a lucky break, Shelby decided reluctantly, because it gave her more privacy, more time alone. She could read in her room. And she could even work late at her typewriter because Pam slept soundly. Nothing would wake her.

With Pam gone most of the time, Shelby didn't have to make small talk or hear about the *millions* of boys Pam knew. But even when Pam was out, Shelby still had to put up with Pam's housekeeping habits.

Pam was—well—a slob, Shelby thought, although she hated to think about her roommate that way. But even the word *slob* seemed to be an understatement. Pam never hung up *anything*, and by the end of the first week, her dresser and chair were heaped chin-high with dirty clothes. The floor around her desk was stacked with books and littered with scraps of paper and half-finished evidence cards. On the shelf over Pam's bed was a dried-up half a hamburger, and a plate of shriveled french fries stuck out from under her bed. Shelby closed her eyes and refused to speculate about where the catsup might be.

Shelby knew she wasn't the neatest person in the world, but she'd learned that it was easier to hang up her skirt than to find it wrinkled. Under other circumstances, she probably would have told Pam how she felt about the mess. But remembering what had happened on their first day together, she tried to hold off as long as she could.

By the end of the week, though, Shelby had

had it. Pam came bursting in, pulled her T-shirt over her head, and flung it on the pile of clothes on her chair. Muttering under her breath, she rummaged through a heap of twice-worn clothes for a clean blouse.

Shelby, who was curled up on her bed reading, spoke up in what she hoped was a mild tone of voice. "Wouldn't it be easier to find things if your clothes were in the closet?" she asked as casually as she could.

Pam sniffed. "You sound just like my older sister," she said crossly. "Boy, will I be glad when she goes off to college this year and I can do whatever I like with my room."

Shelby decided it wouldn't help to say anything else. The only hope, Shelby told herself, was that sooner or later Pam would run out of clean clothes and would have to wash some of the dirty ones. Surely then she'd hang them in the closet or put them in a drawer.

Shelby's feeling of isolation grew stronger every day during that long first week. But she had to admit that a lot of it was her own doing. In the morning she got up early so she could jog around the lake before breakfast. She knew she probably wouldn't meet anybody at that hour of the morning. In the cafeteria she sat by herself in a corner by the window, a book propped up against her milk carton as a signal to others that trespassers in her personal space weren't welcome. And on the first weekend, when nearly everyone else had gone to the meadow by the lake for one of Kelly's famous fried chicken and watermelon picnics, Shelby stayed in her room to get ready for Monday's debate. At least that's what she told herself. But although she spent a great deal of time working on the debate, she spent an equal amount of time thinking about Tom and dreading the Fourth-of-July weekend. Every year they had gone to the Hampton picnic together. Maybe this year she'd stay home, so she wouldn't have to see Tom and Holly together. But maybe, in the last couple of weeks, he'd changed his mind. How did he feel about her now? Could they try again—or was that only an impossible dream?

Chapter Six

The long week and the even longer weekend might have had its lonely moments. But it had one huge benefit, Shelby reminded herself as she walked into the squad room on Monday afternoon. The extra research and practice time had given her confidence. Shelby and Laura were paired against Alex and Pete, and the two girls had practiced together several times so they knew their arguments very well.

"Wonder of wonders, I'm not even nervous," Laura whispered as they took their seats in the front of the room. "Are you?"

Surprised, Shelby paused. "No, not at all," she whispered back. She'd been so busy getting her notes in order and thinking about her presentation that she hadn't had time to worry about being nervous. And even though Matthew was sitting at the back of the room, frowning down at the timer's watch in his hand, she felt surprisingly confident. Win or lose, she knew they'd do a good job.

When it was all over, Shelby and Laura walked jubilantly out of the building toward the Student Union. "Whoopee!" Laura cheered. "Let's toast our success with a chocolate ice-cream soda and a mountain of whipped cream. Hang the calories—just think of all that energy we burned up winning the debate this afternoon."

"Sounds good," Shelby agreed happily, skipping to keep up with her. "After that performance, we deserve a treat."

"Shelby, Laura, wait up!" Taking the steps two at a time, Matthew caught up with them on the sidewalk. He stepped between them and, much to Shelby's surprise, put one arm across each of their shoulders. Suddenly there were goose bumps on Shelby's back. The weight of Matthew's arm felt warm and very good.

"Hey, you two, you were simply terrific!" he exclaimed. "Even Donna was impressed—and that's saying a *whole* lot!"

Laura grinned smugly. "Her Majesty liked it? Well, what did you expect? After all the work we did this weekend, we really deserved to win." She gestured toward Shelby. "Actually, I'll have to admit it's all Shelby's doing.

This girl is one hard worker. She doesn't know when it's time to play. She worked all weekend on our notes."

Shelby ducked her head, conscious of Matthew's eyes on her. "Both of us worked," she said. "Not just me. It takes two on a team to win a debate."

"True enough," Matthew said seriously, but his eyes twinkled. "Did I overhear something about a chocolate ice-cream soda? I could go for that. Keeping the timer's clock is dry work."

"You're on," Laura said. "OK, Shelby?"

"Terrific," Matthew responded promptly before Shelby could say anything. He dropped his arm from her shoulder, and Shelby's suddenly felt cold. She shivered.

After they finished their sodas, Laura looked at her watch. "Oops," she exclaimed hastily. "I promised Pam I'd go into town with her before dinner to shop for a new pair of shorts. Guess I'd better run." She glanced wickedly at Shelby. "See you later, champ," she said with a meaningful smile. "Don't get into trouble without me."

"I'll walk you back across campus, Shelby," Matthew suggested after Laura had gone. "That is, if you're heading back toward the dorms."

"Thanks," Shelby said, wishing fervently

that Laura hadn't made her last remark. "That would be nice." For a few minutes they walked along in silence, the green trees weaving a leafy arch over their heads, bright flowers bordering the neat campus sidewalk.

"I looked for you at Kelly's picnic Sunday afternoon, but I didn't see you anywhere," Matthew said after a long silence. "Did you have an off-campus date or something?"

A day or so before Shelby might have resented the question. But now it seemed very natural, and there wasn't really any point in inventing a reason for not going to the picnic. "No," she said truthfully, not looking at him. "I stayed in my room and worked on the debate." She paused. "Actually, I—I've been feeling kind of out of it for the past week. It's been harder to make friends than I thought, and for some reason, I seem to make enemies quicker than friends." She laughed a little, thinking about Donna and Wendy—and even Pam.

Matthew, suddenly serious, stopped in the middle of the sidewalk and clamped a strong hand on her arm and spun her around. "You can't go on hiding out, Shelby," he said with a fierce intensity that caught Shelby by surprise. "I understand what you're going through because I've been there, too. Last year I wasted the first two weeks of camp moping around and feeling sorry for myself. I missed a lot of fun. Don't let that happen to you."

"Well, it's kind of hard—" Shelby began defensively.

Matthew nodded, looking into her eyes. "Sure it is. But that's no excuse. Everything that's worth doing is hard, isn't it? Getting up in front of those kids and doing a good job in the debate today couldn't have been easy." His eyes held Shelby's, and suddenly her throat felt dry. "And, anyway, you can't spend all your time working. I—I want to have some of it." He looked down at the ground and then smiled, a shy, lopsided smile. "Here I am, a big-timer with words—state debate champ, and all that—and I can't seem to say what I want to say. That I want to be with you. That I think you're somebody pretty special."

For a few seconds, time seemed to freeze around them as Shelby stood still, her heart hammering against her chest and her pulse racing. She tried to speak, but the words wouldn't come out. After a moment Matthew broke the spell by glancing down at his watch.

"Tell you what," he said in a more normal tone of voice. "We've got an hour before the cafeteria opens for supper. I usually go for a quick run around the lake about this time of day." There was a teasing glint in his eyes. "I know you're an early-morning jogger because

I've seen you out the window. Want to try an afternoon run?"

Shelby took a deep breath. *"You can't go on hiding out,"* Matthew had said. He was right. She straightened her shoulders and smiled up at him. "Yes, I'd like to do that," she said happily. "I'll go put on my running shorts and shoes."

"Great," Matthew shot back and squeezed her hand, hard. "Meet you at the footbridge in ten minutes."

As Shelby hurried toward her dorm, she felt almost light-headed with happiness.

The afternoon was cool, and the scent of pines filled the air as they jogged around the lake on the wide gravel path. After forty minutes and two full circles around the lake, Shelby flagged to a panting stop.

"Enough, enough, already," she said, laughing. "I'm used to a little civilized jogging—none of this marathon stuff. Anyway, isn't it time for dinner?" She looked at her watch. "I feel like I could eat a whole cow." This was the first time she had really had any appetite since she arrived at camp.

Matthew looked toward the west, where the sun was beginning to drop toward the hills. "Yep, dinner time," he said with satisfaction. He wiped the sweat off his forehead with one tanned arm and draped the other across her shoulders. "I was going to ask you to eat with me, but I suppose you want to sit in your corner by the window with your book," he said teasingly.

Shelby felt happiness bubbling up inside her. All the time that she had thought she was so alone, Matthew had been noticing her. Playfully, she pulled away from him. "Well," she said slowly as though she were giving the matter deep thought. "Well, I suppose I could eat with you—if you promise not to interrupt my reading."

"You're on," Matthew said over his shoulder as he started up the path. "Last one to the chow line has to carry both trays!"

Later, when she thought back on the next week, Shelby knew that it had been one of the happiest in her life, if only because it stood in such sharp contrast to the loneliness of the week before. After dinner in the cafeteria that night, she and Matthew had walked together to the library. The next morning they had met at dawn for an early-morning run around the lake. Filmy patches of mist floated across the quiet surface of the lake, and the path was damp with dew, but the cool air was exhilarating. "This is a better time than afternoon," Matthew said, panting, as they trotted back to their dorms. "How about tomorrow morning?" Shelby nodded happily, and a wide smile spread over her sun-flushed face.

Now that practice rounds had begun, the most intense research was finished. That meant that everyone could relax a little and enjoy the campus. So one late afternoon in the middle of the second week Matthew rented horses at the college stables, and he and Shelby rode through the quiet woods, enjoying the sound of the wind in the high pines and the soft scrunch of pine needles under the horses' hooves. Another afternoon they went for a refreshing swim in the icy cold lake with Pam and Alex.

By the end of the week Shelby realized to her surprise that she had thought about Tom only a half-dozen times in the past few days, mostly when she remembered the upcoming holiday weekend. The weekend was going to be tough, that was all there was to it. If she went to the Fourth-of-July picnic, she'd be sure to see Tom—after all, it was a tradition. How would he feel when he saw her again? Would Holly be with him?

She pushed the uneasy anticipation out of her mind and thought instead about Matthew and the easy, comfortable friendship that had developed between them. As the week went by, it had given her an entirely different outlook on things. Donna didn't seem like such an ogre any longer. After Shelby and Laura had won their second practice round, she'd even complimented Shelby on the improvement in her debating.

And even Shelby's relationship with Pam seemed to improve. One afternoon Pam came back from taking a shower, her robe clutched around her and a towel wrapped around her dripping hair, and began looking for a clean blouse to wear to dinner. "I can't find *anything* in this mess!" she wailed after a few minutes searching. She looked around at the litter, shaking her head. "How in the world can you put up with me, Shelby?" she asked woefully. "I can't *believe* this rubble. There are clothes and books everywhere!"

Shelby laughed, glancing around. "It *is* pretty bad, isn't it?" She paused, considering. "This time last week I was really upset, maybe because I was spending so much time in the room and I had to look at all this stuff. But this week I've been so busy I haven't had time to notice. Or maybe I'm just getting used to it."

"Well, it's been really nice of you not to yell at me about it," Pam said, looking at her unmade bed. "I guess I'd better give up tennis tonight and clean it up, so we'll at least have room to walk around."

Shelby looked at her in pretend-horror. "Give up tennis for tonight? Clean the room?" She put her hand on Pam's forehead. "Here, let me see if you have a temperature."

Pam laug..ed and playfully pushed her hand away. "Yeah, that *is* kind of drastic, isn't it?" She looked around again. "Maybe I can put it off until tomorrow morning before breakfast. But I promise I'll do better." After that, her habits improved considerably, and Shelby noticed that almost everything she took off eventually found its way back in the closet. And although the desk was still a mess, Pam had picked up most of the papers and books from the floor.

By Friday night the week had gone by so quickly that Shelby could hardly believe that early the next morning her parents were coming to drive her home for the three-day Fourth-of-July weekend. That night she and Matthew met Pam and Alex at the library, and the boys walked the girls back to their dorm.

"I've got a good idea," Matthew suggested. "Let's go down and sit on the bridge. There's a full moon, and since Friday night curfew is late, we don't have to be in for another couple of hours."

"Great idea," Alex said enthusiastically to Pam. "We could even go swimming. How about it, Pam? Ready for a moonlight swim?"

"Not me," Pam answered emphatically. "That water's only about sixty-five degrees—it's cold enough during the day, but it must be agonizing at night. Who needs it?" She looked thoughtfully toward the lighted tennis courts. "However, if you're up to it, Alex, we might try a little tennis. I expect Matthew and Shelby can manage to find the lake by themselves."

"Lady, you haven't felt the full force and power of my magnificent backhand yet," Alex said. "Are you sure you want to test such a devastating weapon at this late hour of the night?"

"That," Pam jeered, "is the dumbest piece of nonsense I've heard all week. Just let me get my racket, and we'll see who's got a magnificent backhand." The two of them vanished in the direction of the dorms, still taunting each other.

"Do you want to get a sweater?" Matthew asked. "I'll wait if you do."

Shelby shook her head and rubbed her arms. The wind was cool, but that wasn't what was making her shiver. "No, I'm just fine," she said.

"I asked Kelly about checking out one of his sailboats next week," Matthew said as they walked along. "He's got a Sunfish at the dock if you'd like to do that."

Shelby nodded. "That sounds like fun. But

you'll have to remember that I've never been sailing. You've got a lot of teaching to do."

"I'll bet you'll be a good learner," Matthew said, taking her hand.

The moon on the lake was almost magical. They sat quietly on the bridge, their feet swinging over the edge, watching the water ripple softly against the shore. The sleeping ducks looked like soft, shadowy mounds of dark feathers among the rocks, and the breeze held the faint fragrance of honeysuckle. After a moment Matthew slipped his arm around Shelby.

"I want you to know how much I—admire you, Shelby," he said quietly. "You're a real winner. I like a girl who knows what she wants and goes after it, the way you have this week. Somehow, I don't think there are many girls like you in the world." In the darkness Shelby felt a warm flush stain her cheeks, and she was glad for the shadows.

After a moment Matthew cupped his fingers under her chin and turned her face toward him. "I want you always to feel like a winner," he said softly, and brushed his lips against hers in a sweet, tender kiss that filled her with warmth and delight. As he put his arms around her, she could feel them trembling almost imperceptibly. His breath was warm against her neck.

"Thank you, Matthew," she whispered. "Thank you." As his lips closed on hers again, it was all she could say.

Chapter Seven

Shelby was filled with excitement and anticipation during the ride home for the holiday weekend. It had been great to see her parents when they had come to pick her up, and she was looking forward to catching up on everything that had happened while she was at camp.

When they drove into Hampton, Shelby was amazed to see that everything looked just the way it had when she left. She knew it was probably silly, but because she felt so different, she somehow expected the world she had left to look different, too. But the streets of Hampton looked just the same: she recognized the cars parked in front of Barney's as they drove by, and she wondered if her friends had been doing the same old things the whole time she'd been gone. And when they finally arrived home and Shelby ran up to her room, everything was just the way she had left it—her stuffed animals, her posters, and her bulletin board, with the gaping holes that had been left when she'd taken down Tom's pictures. She looked at it for few minutes and then moved the other pictures around until the board looked full again.

Roger hadn't changed, either—he was still as inquisitive as ever. "Hey, Shelby, it's great to have you back. Did you get to go horseback riding? How about sailing? Did you win the tournament?"

Shelby looked at her brother affectionately, smiling at his barrage of eager questions. "No, the debate tournament doesn't take place until the last week of the workshop. And, yes, I've been horseback riding. I haven't been sailing yet—but a friend has offered to take me."

As she spoke the word "friend," Shelby felt a rush of warmth inside her. She felt a tingling as she remembered how Matthew had kissed her by the lake the night before. *I like a winner,* he had whispered to her. He had such confidence in her—and in himself. She shook herself and turned back to Roger.

"I'm going to learn how to sail a Sunfish. And when I come home from camp, we'll go out to the lake, and I'll show you how. OK?"

"Wow! Great! Hey, are you going to the fireworks tonight? How about the picnic?" He gave her a knowing grin. "Are you going to see Tom at the park tonight?" With another grin, he was gone.

Shelby's smile faded, and as she unpacked, she tried unsuccessfully to sort out her confused feelings. She wasn't at all sure how she felt about going to the picnic and the fireworks. On one hand, the picnic was a cherished family tradition, as well as a community gathering for the entire town of Hampton. Every year Shelby's mom would fill the wicker picnic basket with crisp fried chicken, creamy potato salad, and sliced tomatoes sprinkled with fresh dill. Dad would brew a huge jug of mint-sprigged iced tea, and he and Roger would make a big batch of vanilla ice cream.

In the park they'd spread out their picnic on a red-and-white-checked tablecloth in the shade of a giant oak tree, just up the hill from the spot where the fireworks always took place. And all around them would be other families. It was almost like an old-fashioned family reunion, Shelby's mom said—but for an extended family. Even if *you* didn't have a very big family, there was always someone at the picnic whom you wanted to see but hadn't seen in a long time, or a great aunt of someone you didn't even know very well, who was wondering if you wanted just one more piece of cake or handful of cherries. The picnic was a time to eat, exchange stories, catch up on gossip—and it was always a lot of fun.

But on the other hand, there was the likelihood that if she went with her parents to the picnic she would see Tom—no, she'd probably see Tom and Holly, who were sure to be there together. Even though the last wonderful week had given her greater confidence in herself and a new perspective on what had happened between Tom and her, she wasn't sure she could trust her emotions. And the picnic was the last place she'd want anyone to see her crying. Shelby went downstairs to find her mother, who was in the kitchen frying chicken.

"You don't have to go if you don't want to, of course," her mother said reasonably. "But don't most of your friends know that you're back home for the holiday? How will you explain to them why you didn't go to the fireworks? And wouldn't Tom get the idea that you're *afraid* to see him?" She smiled warmly at Shelby. "You know, honey, most of the time it's better to meet your problems than to hide from them."

That was what Matthew had said, too, Shelby remembered. And thinking the situation over carefully, she knew that he and her mother were right. She would go to the picnic.

It was a short ride to the park, which was only six blocks from the Scotts' house. Shelby got out of the car and stood looking at the park, unaware of the activities around her. The park held many memories, most of them of Tom. The path down the middle had been their shortcut from grammar school, and she and Tom had walked along it almost every morning and afternoon since first grade. Later, when they got to high school, the park had been a favorite place to go in the evenings. She remembered when Tom had kissed her there one autumn, under the streetlight, in the shadow of the huge maple tree that turned shimmery gold every October. "I'll always love you, Shelby," he had whispered, looking into her eyes, his face framed by the golden autumn leaves behind him. "Nothing will ever change that."

But something *had* changed the way Tom felt about her, and even though Matthew had helped to make things better, Shelby still felt a wrenching loss when she thought about Tom and his arms tight around her, his lips gentle and sweet.

"Hey, how about helping out, daydreamer," Mr. Scott chided. He was carrying the lawn chairs from the car to their picnic spot. "Your mom has the basket of food. Why don't you bring the ice-cream freezer?"

Roger spread the tablecloth out on the grass at the top of the hill, and they all began eating. "Mmm," Shelby murmured happily, finishing a drumstick. "There's nothing like Mom's fried chicken."

"You mean that the college cafeteria doesn't serve food as good as mine?" her mother asked. "I can't imagine why not."

"The food's good," Shelby insisted. "Better than we expected. And a million times better than the food at Hampton High." She reached for another drumstick, just beating Roger to the draw. "But nothing beats home cooking," she added, handing Roger the drumstick, amused by his look of surprise. She looked up just in time to see her mother and father exchange smiles.

After they had eaten, Shelby and her family wandered around, talking with other families, waiting for the sky to get dark enough for the fireworks. Uneasily, Shelby watched for Tom, but she didn't see him, and after a while she relaxed. Maybe he wasn't there after all, she thought, and she wasn't sure whether she felt relieved or disappointed.

Several of her other friends from the debate club were there, and they all came over to talk. Shelby was glad to see them, but she couldn't get over the feeling that something important had changed—that she had grown while they had stayed the same. Marge, for instance, had been one of her best friends all year. Marge was a member of the debate club, too, even though she hadn't been very serious about it. But in spite of her friendship with Marge, Shelby was having a hard time explaining about camp.

"What's it like being on a college campus?" Marge asked curiously.

Shelby considered. "Well, it's a lot like school," she said finally. "We go to classes in the mornings and afternoons and spend the evenings in the library."

Marge shook her head. "Doesn't sound like much fun to me."

"Maybe it's not everybody's idea of fun," Shelby conceded, thinking of her question to Matthew on the first day. "But the kids who go to camp are pretty serious about debate, and they're willing to work. Most of them, that is," she amended. She couldn't exactly say that Pam was serious about debate.

"Well, better you than me, I guess," Marge retorted. She glanced enviously at Shelby. "Next year you'll probably walk away with all the tournaments."

After Marge had gone, Shelby was left with an odd feeling, as though something familiar and comfortable had come to an end while she wasn't looking.

But her thoughts were interrupted by a firm hand on her shoulder. Mr. Lawsen, her debate coach, had come over to say hello. "We're all expecting you to do a good job in the tournament in a couple of weeks," he said, smiling at Shelby. "In fact, I'm planning to come to see you debate in the final round."

Disconcerted, Shelby replied hastily, "Thanks, Mr. Lawsen, but I don't think you ought to plan on the trip. There are some really good debaters at camp, and this is only my first year." She thought of Matthew and added firmly, "In fact, I don't think there's a chance in the world that I'll make it into the championship round."

"Just the same," Mr. Lawsen said stubbornly, "I want you to know I'm coming." He patted her arm confidently. "I know you'll do a good job, Shelby. All you have to do is decide that you want to win."

Shelby tried not to let her real feelings show as she thanked her coach and said goodbye. *If only it could be that simple,* she thought to herself wistfully.

Soon the fireworks began and everyone settled down to watch. Every year's fireworks seemed better than the last ones, Shelby thought as she watched fiery starbursts trailing ribbons of brilliantly colored diamonds across the black sky. But every other year Tom had been beside her, and they had held hands and watched together. Now Shelby sat alone, a little away from her family, in a comfortable grassy spot she and Tom had found years before.

The fireworks were nearly over when Shelby heard what she'd been half hoping for. "Hello, Shelby."

Startled, she tried to keep calm. "Hello, Tom," she said, looking up and trying to subdue the sudden flutter she felt inside.

She could see his silhouette against the night sky. "Can I sit down for a minute?" he asked. He was trying to appear casual, but Shelby could hear the uncertainty in his voice.

"Sure." Shelby shifted to make room for him, and Tom sat down beside her. She could smell his familiar scent, and it made her heart beat faster.

"Pretty nice fireworks," Tom said after an awkward pause.

"Yes, I think they're even better than they were last year," Shelby said and then stopped quickly.

"Yeah." There was another long pause, and then Tom asked quietly, "How do you like debate camp? Are you having a good time?"

Shelby hesitated. She might as well be honest about it. "I really like what we're doing," she said. "Laura—my partner—and I won a couple of practice rounds last week." She picked up a pebble and turned it over in her hand, feeling its smooth roundness. "It's neat to work with Laura. She's not afraid to win. *There*, she thought. *It's out.*

Tom shifted abruptly, and even in the dark, Shelby could feel a different tension in his body. But what came next was completely unexpected.

"Do you think things might be any different between us if we tried again, Shelby?"

There was a brilliant starburst overhead, and it seemed to match the bursting happiness in Shelby as she turned to Tom. "Do you really mean it?" she asked. And then she sobered. "What about—what about Holly?"

Tom hesitated. "I'm still seeing her once in a while," he said. "But if you and I could be—well, if we could go back together again, I'd be willing . . ." His voice trailed off, and he took a deep breath and started again. "If you and I could be together again, the way we used to be before all this—this other stuff began, I'd stop seeing Holly." He leaned toward her, and his voice was urgent. "How about it, Shelby?"

"Oh, yes, Tom," she said happily. "Oh, yes, yes!" She shivered with delight as Tom's arms went around her in a familiar embrace. She'd been so wrong. Nothing had changed after all!

"My, you're up early," Mrs. Scott observed as Shelby walked into the kitchen the next morning already dressed. "You're learning some new habits at camp, I see."

Shelby giggled. "Tom's coming in a few minutes, and we're going to ride out to the lake."

Mrs. Scott looked up quickly from the legal papers she had spread across the kitchen table. "So you two have made up your differences?" There was a sharp question in her voice.

Shelby smiled dreamily. "Everything's going to be just the way it was before. Oh, Mom, I'm so happy!"

Shelby's mother hesitated. "Think hard, Shelby," she urged, her face serious. "Don't give up what you've gained."

Shelby looked at her mother. What did she mean? But there wasn't time to ask because Tom was at the door, anxious to leave.

They rode their bikes out to the sandy beach at Lake Hampton and spent the day lying lazily in the sun, taking turns rubbing lotion on each other's shoulders and dipping in the cold water. Marge and Howie, her boyfriend, joined them in the afternoon, and that evening they all went to Barney's for hamburgers. Everyone was there, and Shelby felt a distinct pleasure as she walked in with Tom. Now they would all know that she and Tom were together and that everything was right again.

They said good night on the front porch. "Tomorrow you go back to camp," Tom said, sitting down beside Shelby on the steps. He sounded disgruntled. "I wish you could stay here."

"But I'm looking forward to going back," Shelby said, surprised. "The elimination rounds are coming up and then the big tournament. I'm sure I won't win, but it will be a lot of fun, anyway." It *would* be fun, she thought with happy anticipation. "And it will be good practice for next year."

"Next year?" Tom swung around sharply to face her.

"Well, of course," Shelby answered, puzzled. "I've really learned a lot about debating. It'll be a big help in next year's competition."

Tom's eyes grew steely. "But we *agreed*," he said flatly.

"Agreed to what?"

"Agreed that things would go back the way they were before all this debate stuff got in the way. Last night when I said I wanted to go back together, I said it had to be the way it *was*." He slipped his arm around Shelby's

shoulders and dropped his voice to a concilia-
tory murmur. "Please, Shelby, let's don't start
arguing again. It's been such a great day—I
don't want to spoil it."

Shelby pulled away. "But I don't understand, Tom. You mean, you don't want us to
be in debate together next year? You don't
want *me* to be in debate?" She tried frantically
to remember what Tom had said the night
before, but all she could remember was the
exploding happiness she had felt when he'd
said he wanted to get back together.

"Yes, that's what I meant," he said reasonably. "And you agreed."

"No, I didn't," Shelby insisted. "At least, I
didn't realize that I was agreeing to anything
like *that*." She stopped. Everything was falling
apart again, and she couldn't stop it. But suddenly she knew she didn't want to. *"I want
you always to feel like a winner,"* Matthew
had said. He believed in her—he wasn't
threatened by her success. But Tom wasn't
confident enough even to let her be a competi-
tor. "I *can't* agree, Tom," she said softly, looking away from him.

Tom stood up and thrust his hands into his
pockets. He looked like a hurt, disappointed
child, Shelby realized suddenly. "If that's the
way you feel, then there isn't any point in
going on with this." He hesitated for a

moment as though he were waiting for her to contradict him.

Shelby stood up, too. "No, there isn't," she agreed. She stood on tiptoe and kissed him gently on the cheek. "I—I guess we just outgrew each other, Tom," she whispered. "The way we outgrew the tree house." And then she turned and went into the house, leaving Tom staring after her.

Chapter Eight

"Are you sure that you want to go back by yourself?" Shelby's mother asked as Shelby got ready to climb on board the bus that would take her back to Northwestern State. "We *can* take you back to the campus, you know."

"You've always wanted me to be independent, Mom," Shelby replied with a new decisiveness. She squeezed her mother's hand. "And it's easier for me to go on the bus than for you and Dad to drive me all the way up there and then drive back again."

Her mother smiled. "You're right," she agreed pleasantly. "Both of us are really busy at the office—we've got a big case coming to trial next week." She gave Shelby a quick, hard hug. "I'm glad to see you doing things on your own, Shelby. Have a good trip back, and we'll see you at the tournament."

"Now, Mom, don't expect too much," Shelby warned. "Chances are that I'll end up in the consolation rounds."

"I'm not expecting too much," her mother replied confidently. She smiled. "I know what your capabilities are."

As the bus pulled away, Shelby shook her head in exasperation. Mr. Lawsen, her parents, Matthew—everyone except Tom—had such high expectations for her, which, actually, made her feel good. It was nice to know there were people who believed in her. If Tom had really loved her, she thought, he would have wanted the best for her—the best for both of them.

Settling into her seat for the hour-long bus ride, Shelby looked absently out the window as the trees and houses sped by. She hadn't exactly looked forward to the weekend, but now she knew that going home had been good. It had given her a chance to measure how much she had changed. And it had given her a chance to measure Tom, too. Yes, she still cared about him. But now she could see their relationship in a different perspective. It *had* been real, and important, and right for its place and time. But during those two short weeks at camp, she'd changed. She'd become more self-confident, more independent. And there wasn't anything wrong with that, she reminded herself, thinking how popular and yet how determined Laura was. One of the most important lessons she'd learned was that if Tom couldn't deal with the change in her, the relationship couldn't grow. And it was wrong to hold on to a relationship that would keep either one of them back, keep either one of them from growing.

But what about Matthew? How did he fit into her life? She still wasn't sure. His kiss under the spell of the magical silver moonlight had been special, she had to admit. But it was too soon to tell what might happen between them. But still, she softened and warmed when she thought of him, and the lines of his face in her memory were clear and bright. She could hardly wait to see him when she got back to camp.

But she didn't see him that evening. He must have returned late, she thought. And although she looked all over the dining room, the next morning, she didn't see him either. She waited by the meal-ticket checker's table for a long time, trying to swallow the disappointment rising in her throat. Finally she got her tray and went to eat with Pam and Alex, who were hunched glumly over their breakfasts, looking as though they wished they were someplace else.

"Well, how was your weekend, Shelby?" Alex

asked with a strained smile. "Did you wow all the homefolks with tales of your miraculous debate victories?"

Sitting down, Shelby flipped a cornflake at him and laughed. What was wrong with Alex this morning? she wondered. "I didn't have to," she said, shrugging. "Hampton rolled out the red carpet for me—why, they even shot off a whole hour's worth of fireworks in my honor. And they held a picnic for me, too." She began to eat.

"Now, there's an odd coincidence for you," Pam said, poking her soft-boiled egg. "*My* hometown gave me a fireworks reception, too, and I didn't even win any debates." She looked up and sighed distractedly. "In fact, if I don't do better this week, my squad leader just might send me home in disgrace. I'm way behind on my evidence assignments, and I didn't do so well in the practice rounds last week. I thought I'd catch up this weekend, but—"

"The spirit was willing, but the old sense of discipline was a little weak," Alex finished for her. He picked up her hand and examined her calloused palm. "Don't tell me, let me guess. You spent most of your time playing tennis, and you didn't even go near the library. Right?"

Pam heaved a dramatic sigh. "Well, actually,

I *did* practice a lot of self-discipline this weekend—but it was on the tennis court, not in the library, I'm afraid." She paused and looked more cheerful. "But my backhand's looking a lot stronger."

Alex grinned and spread jam on his toast. "Sounds just like me. But at least we get to start over again this week with a brand-new squad leader. It's like getting a second lease on life, after Donna's dictatorship."

Pam nodded emphatically, and her face brightened. "I'll be glad to make a switch, too, even though my squad leader hasn't been as tough as yours. Who knows? Maybe I'll get somebody with some compassion. Maybe I'll even get somebody who cares about tennis."

Shelby, who had been only half listening to the conversation, glanced up sharply. "Switch squad leaders?" Then, with a sinking feeling, she remembered what Donna had told them at the beginning of the workshop. "Does that mean that everybody will be assigned to a different squad?" she asked. She thought of Matthew. If they got reassigned, she wouldn't be able to see him as much as before. The disappointment was so strong that she suddenly wasn't hungry. She pushed her cereal bowl away.

"You got it," Alex said with grim satisfaction. "Dr. Lewis is making the new assignments this morning at assembly. That means everybody gets a fresh start." He gave a dispirited chuckle. "And some of us really need it."

Before assembly began Shelby looked around anxiously for Matthew, but again she couldn't find him. Nevertheless, she saved the empty seat beside her on the aisle, just in case he came in later. Dr. Lewis welcomed everyone back and then announced that the new squad assignments would be ready by the end of the morning's lecture.

"We're moving people into groups according to ability," she said as she opened her lecture notes. "We hope that your second squad assignments will be more challenging than your first ones."

Next to Shelby, Pam muttered, "More challenging? Who does she think she's kidding? Any more challenge and I'm out of business."

The lecture was half over when Matthew slipped into the seat next to her. Shelby looked up in pleased surprise, and he smiled back, his blue eyes warm.

"It's good to see you, Shelby," he whispered, giving her fingers a quick, affectionate squeeze. And then in a lower whisper, "I missed you."

A sparkling happiness burst through Shelby, and her heart did a dozen joyful somersaults. "I missed you, too," she whispered back. Matthew's eyes held hers, and she felt so open and transparent that she was sure he could read everything that was going through her mind. Quickly she dropped her glance.

In a minute he let her hand go, but she could still feel the warm pressure of his fingers. "Can I see your notes after the lecture?" he asked in a more businesslike tone. "I need to know what I missed while I was helping with the new squad assignments."

Shelby nodded. So that's where he'd been. She might have known that he'd be involved in helping with the new assignments.

"By the way," he whispered casually as he flipped open his notebook and reached into his shirt pocket for his pen, "you got assigned to one of the advanced squads."

Shelby looked up in utter amazement. "Advanced? I did? But I'm not good en—"

"Yes, you are. According to *Donna*, anyway," Matthew retorted. He cocked one eyebrow, and an amused sparkle glinted in his eyes. "Are you going to dispute your squad leader's expert evaluation of your debating skills?" He turned sternly to his notebook. "Now pay attention to the lecture. Your new squad leader will probably give you a quiz on it."

After the lecture was finished, Matthew

helped distribute the new assignment sheets. When Shelby got hers, she scanned it breathlessly. Matthew had been right, she saw with a sudden exhilaration. She'd been assigned to a group with seven others who had won their practice debates, under a squad leader named Brian, who according to the dormitory gossip was absolutely the best leader at camp. She scanned the names of her squad again. She didn't see . . .

"Oh, no," Pam moaned. "I don't believe it!"

"What's the matter?" Shelby asked, concerned. In her anxiety to find out the squad she'd been assigned to, she'd almost forgotten about her friend. "Can't you find your name on the list?"

"Oh, I've found it, all right," Pam exploded. "But I might as well go home right now." She pointed dramatically to the list. "I've got Donna!"

Shelby smothered a giggle and then immediately felt guilty. Poor Pam. No question about it, the change to a more demanding squad leader was going to be awfully hard for her. "Well, it's really not so bad," she replied sympathetically, giving Pam's arm an encouraging squeeze. "Donna will make sure you know your stuff. She may be tough, but she's fair, and she'll make sure that you know what you're doing." As she heard herself speak, she realized that she was grateful to Donna for setting such high standards—standards she might never have set for herself.

Pam wasn't paying any attention. "But you never had a *minute* of free time the last two weeks," she complained. "When am I going to find time to work on tennis? And the tournament begins right after I get back! I've *got* to have time to practice!"

Shelby nodded understandingly. "You do have a problem," she agreed, trying to calm Pam down. "But Donna's a pretty good squad leader, once you get used to her."

Pam still looked stunned. "Do you think there'd be any chance of getting the assignment changed?" she asked hopefully. "Maybe if I went to Dr. Lewis. . . ." After a minute she closed her eyes and shook her head despairingly. "No, they'd never let me," she moaned. "If they let people transfer out of Donna's squad, she wouldn't have any squad members left. Everybody would leave!"

On the way out of the assembly hall, Shelby looked down at her list again. No, she'd been right the first time, Matthew's name wasn't there. He was still assigned to Donna's squad.

"Well, what do you think of your new squad leader?" Matthew asked as they finished their late-afternoon jog around the lake. He reached for her hand, nodding toward a huge fallen tree lying in a grassy spot just off the trail. "Let's go sit on that log for a few minutes and catch our breath." Matthew brushed the log off, and they sat down side by side.

"We didn't have a lot of time with the group today because we were so late getting started. We just introduced ourselves. But I think I'm really going to like him," Shelby said happily. "What about you? You're still working with Donna's squad. What do you think of the new group?"

Matthew scowled, and his blue eyes were dark behind his glasses. "Well, we didn't get off to a very good start today. Some of the debaters don't seem very serious. Pam, for instance." He glanced at Shelby. "Can *you* do anything about Pam? Maybe, since she's your roommate, she'll listen to you."

Shelby laughed helplessly. "I don't think anybody can do anything about Pam. She's kind of—well, you know. She's really wrapped up in her tennis, and she's just not very interested in debate. I think she even wishes she hadn't come."

"Yeah, I've noticed," Matthew answered thoughtfully. "And Donna's noticed, too. She's going to come down hard if Pam doesn't straighten up."

"I know how *that* feels," Shelby said,

remembering how she had felt the first time she met Donna. "I can't promise anything, but I'll see what I can do."

After a minute Matthew stood up and pulled her to her feet, and they started down the trail toward the lake. "I've been meaning to ask you something else," he said casually. "Do I remember your saying that you were in a paired debate last year?"

Shelby frowned. Thinking about the debate and its aftermath was still painful. "Yes, I was," she said hesitantly. "Why?"

"Oh, no special reason," Matthew said carelessly, taking her hand. After a minute he added, "Paired debating is part of the tournament, you know. Dr. Lewis picks a couple of the best debaters to challenge each other. It's a big honor to be chosen."

Shelby nodded. "Yes, I know. I've heard about it." She looked down at their intertwined fingers, and her hand felt warm and comfortable in Matthew's.

"Did you enjoy the paired debate?" he persisted.

Shelby thought for a minute. It was hard to separate the pleasure of the debate itself from the pain of her split with Tom. "I really liked the debate." "If only my opponent hadn't been so—"

"Hadn't been so what?"

"Hadn't been—so well-prepared," Shelby finished. Somehow, she just couldn't bring herself to tell Matthew about the debate and about Tom. Anyway, it was all finished and over now. There wasn't any reason to talk about it. Matthew shot her a curious glance, and she added hurriedly, "But I *did* enjoy paired debating. It's a real challenge to debate alone."

Matthew nodded. "Yes, that's the best part of it for me, too," he replied. "It's sort of like the difference between playing singles and doubles. In doubles, you've always got a back-up. In singles, you're out there all by yourself, and there's nobody to pick up the shots you drop." There was a peculiar glint in his eyes, and then he changed the subject abruptly. "There we go, talking about tennis again. Doesn't anybody around here ever think about anything else?"

"Well, how about sailing?" Shelby ventured. "Seems to me I remember that somebody promised me a sailboat lesson this week."

Matthew grinned. "You've read my mind. Let's go see if we can get one for tomorrow afternoon." His blue eyes sized her up. "Let's see whether you're as good a sailor as you are a debater." He stood up and started down the path.

"I hope you're not expecting a lot," Shelby

protested as she trotted along after him. "After all, I've never been sailing before."

Matthew wheeled around to confront her on the narrow path, and she nearly bumped into him. "Of course I'm expecting a lot," he said, his eyes dancing. "I'm expecting a winner."

Chapter Nine

After the previous week's practice rounds, Shelby had been pretty sure where she stood in Donna's squad. But in her new group she felt uncertain and a little bit anxious. All these kids seemed to have a lot more debate experience than the ones in Donna's group—and much more confidence in their abilities. And they all looked interested and serious. They didn't seem at all concerned about the amount of work that Brian was describing to them.

Brian was a slender, brown-haired boy with quick, penetrating brown eyes and an impish grin. "Most of your research was supposed to have been finished last week," he told them. "Everybody ought to have a couple hundred evidence cards by now. In fact, you probably need an index just to keep them straight."

"What we *really* need is a wheelbarrow,"

said one of the girls, a petite redhead. Everybody laughed in agreement. "These file boxes are getting awfully heavy to lug around!"

"Well, you can always leave them here in the squad room and just take the ones you're working on, Maria," Brian pointed out. He went around the table, giving everyone a typed schedule for the next few days.

"During our work sessions this week, we'll spend most of the time doing practice debates and evaluations."

Marty, a tall, broad-shouldered boy with a booming voice, raised his hand. "What about the tournament, Brian?" he asked. "When will the teams be announced?"

Brian grinned. "Getting anxious, huh? The tournament begins a week from Thursday, as you probably remember. There'll be three rounds and two brackets, the championship bracket and the consolation bracket. That means that everybody gets to keep on debating—win or lose." One of the boys at the end of the table snickered, and Brian looked up without expression. "Of course, I don't expect anybody in this group to lose. You'll all end up in the championship bracket. Right?" He waited expectantly, and when nobody said anything, he frowned. "I said you're all winners—right?"

This time there was an enthusiastic chorus of "Right!" Brian nodded in satisfaction and went on. "Dr. Lewis will post the list of teams in a day or two, together with the names of the two who are chosen to do the pair debating. Anybody else have questions about the tournament?"

He looked around the table. "OK, gang, let's get started. At the end of today's session, I'll announce teams for tomorrow's practice round."

Even though she was impatient for it to end, the long session went quickly for Shelby. Brian seemed to be much more flexible than Donna. But actually, as Shelby thought about it, she decided that Donna had been an excellent squad leader *because* she'd been so tough. It wasn't easy to impress her, and when Shelby had done a good job, she'd felt terrific about it.

At the end of the afternoon, she was pleased to find herself teamed for the next day's practice debate with Marty, who seemed confident and eager.

"We've still got a couple of hours before supper," Marty said as everybody got ready to leave. "Let's work here for a while and go over each other's arguments."

"I'm sorry, Marty." Shelby shook her head quickly. "It'll have to be tonight after dinner— I've already made plans for the rest of the afternoon." This was the afternoon that she and Matthew were going sailing.

Marty nodded. "OK, then how about seven, at the library? We can decide how we're going to handle tomorrow's opening arguments."

"Sounds good," Shelby said. She hesitated. "I hope I'll do a good job tomorrow," she said slowly. "I wouldn't want to keep you from—"

Marty laughed heartily. "I wouldn't worry about that," he said. "The shoe just might be on the other foot, as they say."

The late-afternoon sun was golden on the water when Shelby met Matthew at the dock for her sailing lesson. She had pulled on a sleek blue, one-piece swimsuit and a pair of shorts over it. Matthew was already there, standing barefoot beside a small, tipsy-looking boat that rode lightly on the waves. He was dressed in cutoffs, and his familiar red T-shirt. A twisted red bandanna kept his hair out of his eyes.

"We're all set," he said, gesturing toward the boat. "All we have to do is rig it, and we're ready to go."

"It looks kind of small," Shelby replied, gazing at it with concern. "Are you sure it's big enough for the two of us—when one of us doesn't know the first thing about sailing?"

Matt squeezed her arm and laughed. "It'll be

111

a little cozy, maybe, but there's nothing wrong with that. All ready for your lesson?"

Shelby nodded. "Just as long as you remember that I've never been in a sailboat in my life. I don't know port from starboard."

"You don't really have to, as long as you know right from left." Matthew grinned. "We'll just stick to the basics for a while."

Matthew showed her how to pull up the single, large sail that powered the boat. He inserted a slender, dagger-shaped board through the bottom of the boat. "That's our keel," he explained. "It stabilizes the boat and helps to balance the weight of the wind in the sail." He put a hand on the back of her neck and turned her head firmly in the direction he was pointing. "See that long heavy pole attached to the bottom of the sail?"

Shelby nodded, terribly conscious of the warmth of Matthew's fingers against her skin. "The thing that's kind of swinging back and forth?"

"Yeah. And, boy, can it ever swing. It's called the boom, and it'll really give you a headache if it happens to swing into your head. That's why when the skipper's ready to change direction, he yells 'Ready about,' and you duck under the boom as it swings over. Got it?"

Shelby eyed the boom apprehensively for a moment and then pointed to what appeared to be a long stick angling out from the back of the boat. "Is that what you steer with?" she asked. She leaned over and put one foot in the boat, which began to rock violently from side to side.

"Hey, hold on!" Matthew warned, pulling her back. "You can't get into a small boat like that. You'll tip it over. Here, watch me." Carefully he put one foot into the exact center of the boat, then shifted his weight until both feet were in and he was crouched under the boom. The boat hardly rocked at all. He stood up carefully and stepped back onto the dock. "Now, you try it," he instructed.

Shakily, Shelby put one foot into the middle of the boat, but when she brought her other leg inside, she managed to catch a line with the toe of her sneaker and lost her balance. Both arms flailing wildly, she sat down with a crash in the bottom of the boat. The small craft teetered wildly as she grabbed for the sides and tried to duck the swinging boom.

"Neat trick," Matthew said, leaning over to grab the mast and steady it. "Lesson number one in sailing—always watch your feet."

Carefully, Shelby extricated herself from the coiled line that had tripped her up, trying to keep the boat level in the water. "Every time I make a move the boat rocks," she complained.

"Sure it does," Matthew agreed pleasantly,

loosening the mooring line. "That's what makes it so much fun to sail. It's like riding a skittish horse." He grinned as Shelby tried to look unconcerned. "Or walking a tightrope in a high wind." He settled himself at the stern and pushed away from the dock. "OK, Shel, here we go."

The afternoon was marvelous, and Shelby knew that she would remember it forever. The water was so clear she could see the fish swimming lazily among the underwater grasses, and once she saw a giant turtle, trailed by three smaller turtles, paddling along the shore. The breeze was gentle and consistent, and the water lapped quietly against the hull as they sailed along in a companionable silence. After a while Matthew spoke. "Having fun, Shelby?"

Shelby dipped her fingers in the water and looked back at him. He was sprawled comfortably in the stern with the tiller in his hand, shading his eyes with his other hand. "Oh, yes," she answered happily. The sun and the gentle lapping of the water against the sides of the boat were making her drowsy.

"How about sailing the boat for a while?"

Shelby shook her head. "You make it look easy, but I know it isn't," she said. "Don't forget that you've got a real novice on your hands."

Matthew adjusted his headband. "Well, it doesn't take long to get to be an expert," he observed. "I won the regatta back home last weekend, and I've only been sailing for a couple of months."

"I'm impressed," Shelby replied, smiling. She watched the easy, effortless grace of his movements for a few minutes, thinking how well he performed at everything he tried. She added in a low voice, "You must be very competitive."

Matthew nodded slowly, considering. "Yeah, sure, I like to win, no question about it. Doesn't everybody?" He looked questioningly at her. "I know you do—I could see it in the way you handled yourself last week. You're the kind of girl who—" He hesitated, then changed the subject abruptly. "Come on, Shelby, take the tiller. You'll never know whether you can do it unless you try."

"Well, OK," Shelby agreed reluctantly. She got up and began moving awkwardly toward him. "Are you *really* sure you want to do this?"

"Sure, I'm sure." Matthew shifted toward the bow of the boat, still holding on to the tiller. "Now, be careful," he warned. "Move slowly."

As he reached out his hand to steady her, an

unexpected puff of wind hit the back of the sail, and the boom started to swing over.

"Watch out!" Matthew yelled and dived for the wildly swinging boom. Shelby frantically tried to regain her balance. The next moment she and Matthew were both in the cold water, and the boat was on its side, its white hull gleaming, its sail billowing as it bobbed up and down in the water.

"Oh, Matthew, I'm so sorry," Shelby sputtered contritely, spitting out a mouthful of water. "I didn't mean—"

"Hey, no problem," Matthew said. He swam toward the boat. "It wouldn't be a good sail if we didn't get wet." He reached high up on the hull, grabbed the wire side-stay that secured the mast, and pulled the boat toward him. It righted itself gracefully, the sail swinging back and forth. Effortlessly, Matthew hoisted himself into the boat and reached over the side for Shelby's hand.

"When I say 'careful,' I mean *careful*," he said and laughed down at her. "Now that you've shown me how well you can swim, maybe you'd like to try sailing again." He pulled her over the side like a huge wet fish, and she lay, gasping, in the bottom of the boat.

"Ready to take the tiller?"

"You mean you'd still let me sail the boat after I capsized us?"

"What's a little capsize between friends?" Matthew said gallantly, wringing out his sopping shirt. "And, anyway, now you know how to get the boat up again after a capsize. That's a valuable lesson in itself. No extra charge." He patted the seat in the stern of the boat and grinned. "Now come on—try again."

The capsize was only the first of a series of mishaps that Matthew accepted with patient good humor. After Shelby took the tiller, she let the boom swing around quickly, hitting Matthew on the shoulder with a loud *whack*. A few minutes later she narrowly missed a collision with two unsuspecting teenagers in a paddleboat. And in another fifteen minutes she had dropped their paddle overboard, hopelessly tangled a coil of nylon line, and pulled the swivel fitting out of the tiller.

Finally Matthew moved toward the stern. "I think that's enough of a lesson for one day," he said, taking the tiller. "You're about to wear your teacher out with all these catastrophes."

Shelby inched forward, careful not to rock the boat. "Well, you asked for it," she retorted weakly. "I told you I was a novice at sailing."

"Actually, I'm glad you're a novice at something *I'm* good at," Matthew responded. "It's real tough on a debater when his girlfriend is just as good as he is."

Shelby swiveled around suddenly, and the boat rocked. Had he really called her 'his girlfriend'? "Oops, sorry," she muttered, settling down. Matthew had said the same thing about competition that Tom had said. It was hard for two friends to compete with each other. But there was a difference. A *big* difference. Tom had been defensive about their competition. But there wasn't a trace of defensiveness in Matthew's voice. Instead, there was a lighthearted acceptance of it—and something that sounded almost like pride. After a moment she remarked thoughtfully, "I'm *not* just as good as you are at debating, you know."

Matthew shook his head. "When I watched you debate last week, I could see that you're just as good as any of us on the team that won at State." He grinned. "That's why I'm glad that you're such a *klutz* when it comes to sailing. It gives me something to feel superior about."

Chapter Ten

When Shelby got back to her room, she was surprised to find Pam there, hunched over her desk, the curtains tightly drawn against the late-afternoon sun. "It's such a marvelous day, I thought you'd be out playing tennis," Shelby said in surprise. She sat down on her bed and pulled off her sneakers, still wet from the capsize.

Pam shook her head. Her face was strained and anxious. "I knew it'd be a disaster the minute I saw that I'd been assigned to Donna's squad," she said. She held out a long sheet of paper. "But I never figured it would be *this* bad. Look at this list of assignments! How in the world did you stand it for two whole weeks?"

Shelby took off her wet clothes and wrapped herself in her robe. "It really didn't seem so bad," she began. She wanted to add that probably *any* assignment would seem like too much work to Pam. Instead she just continued, "Though some of the other kids did feel that the assignments were pretty heavy—"

"Pretty heavy! She's assigned us thirty evidence cards for tomorrow, and she still expects me to turn in everything that was due to my other squad leader last week. Honestly, Shelby, I'll never catch up!"

"Sure you will," Shelby said comfortingly, remembering her promise to Matthew. Perhaps this was her chance to help out. She went to the drawer and pulled out a pair of clean white shorts and a blue-and-white polo shirt, then grabbed a towel. "I'm going to take a shower now. I told Marty I'd meet him after dinner to work on tomorrow's practice debate. But I could help you for a little while if you want."

"Would you mind terribly? Listen, I'm going to skip dinner and go over to the library. When you get finished, why don't you meet me there? Maybe you can help me locate a couple of pieces of evidence that I've *got* to dig out for my argument."

"OK. I'll meet you about six-thirty."

Pam nodded resignedly. "And if you've got any surefire shortcuts for putting together an argument, bring them with you. I need to find a way to handle all this stuff in a *hurry*."

Shelby shook her head as she left the room. Pam's two weeks on the tennis courts had caught up with her, and she wasn't taking it very well.

"Thanks for coming," Pam whispered as Shelby sat down next to her at the study table.

"I know we're not supposed to eat in the library, but I thought you might be hungry, so I smuggled you something to eat," Shelby whispered back. She opened her book bag. "How about ham and swiss on rye?"

"Gosh, Shelby, you're terrific," Pam answered, snatching the sandwich. She looked around furtively. "Let me know if anybody comes."

"How're you doing?" Shelby asked as Pam attacked the sandwich. The table was littered with books and magazines, and there was an untidy stack of file cards at Pam's right elbow.

Pam smiled ruefully. "Just about the way you'd expect," she conceded, her mouth full. "I've got most of the argument ready for tomorrow, but I can't seem to find the exact piece of evidence I need to clinch the thing."

"What are you looking for?" Shelby asked. "Maybe I've got something in my evidence cards that will help."

"I'm arguing that the federal government

ought to take over the airline industry because a takeover would mean more job security for airline employees." She shook her head and riffled frantically through the pages of a magazine. "I *know* I saw that point made here someplace," she insisted. "I even paper-clipped a note on the front of the magazine so I'd remember where it was. But now that I need it, I can't find it. Why, oh, *why*, didn't I write down the name of the magazine when I had it in front of me?"

Shelby looked puzzled. "I've been all through every one of these magazines, Pam, and I don't remember seeing anything like that. But you're right—it would be a really good piece of evidence if you could find it. We're all debating the same topic—and it sure would make *my* argument a lot tighter."

There was a brief moment of silence. "Maybe there's another way," Pam said thoughtfully. "Since I *know* that quote exists, even if I can't lay my hands on it right this minute, maybe I could just—just make up the name of a magazine." She watched Shelby's face as if she were measuring her response. "Do you think anybody would catch on?"

"If you mean, would Donna know that you're fabricating evidence, I'd have to bet she would. And she's really a nut about that. She gave us a lecture about it once. She says it's the absolute worst thing a debater can do. She even said she'd send someone home for fabbing evidence."

Pam fiddled with her pencil. "Well, I wouldn't really be fabricating evidence," she said evasively, not meeting Shelby's eyes. "I *know* I read that piece somewhere—I just can't locate it now, that's all. It's just a matter of—of thinking up a plausible reference, that's all."

Shelby shook her head again. "Doesn't sound like a good idea to me, Pam," she said firmly. "Anyway, there are lots of other ways to approach that argument. Have you tried . . . ?"

For the next half hour, the two girls worked together, and by the time Shelby left, she thought that Pam had solved most of her problems. "There, you see, it wasn't so bad after all," she said. She pushed her chair back, stood up, and stretched. "You're almost ready for your first practice round tomorrow. All you have to do is practice your opening argument. With another couple hours' work—"

"Gosh, thanks, Shelby," Pam interrupted gratefully, closing her book. "I'm not caught up yet, but things are a lot better than they were." She glanced at her watch. "Hey, look, it's only seven," she said excitedly. "If I get a move on, maybe I can get in an hour's worth of tennis. Alex said he'd play with me."

Shelby shook her head gravely, thinking about what Matthew had said. "Listen, Pam, things are different now that you're in Donna's squad. She insists that everyone spend all evening in the library, and she's got a way of knowing about it if you don't. And there's no place to hide out on a tennis court. She's sure to spot you. Don't you think you ought to lay off tennis until you get home? It's only another couple of weeks."

Pam nodded soberly. "I know. But I've *got* to do a good job in the tennis tournament, Shelby. If I do, they'll offer me a job as a tennis coach at the club. And that means a good shot at a tennis scholarship to college." She looked down at the note cards strewn across the table. "Actually, if you want to know the truth, I think coming to debate camp was a terrible mistake. I should have stayed home and worked on my backhand." She sighed and began to gather up the cards. "At this point, I just want to do enough to get by and take off as much time as I can for tennis. After all, I'm doing what I want to. And you can't be good at everything. Right?"

Shelby nodded. "Right," she agreed, remembering her disastrous sailing experience. "And it's a good thing, too," she added, smiling.

Later that evening Shelby and Matthew sat on a bench in the bowling alley in the Student Union. They were eating hamburgers and french fries while waiting for Kelly to tell them when the next lane was open. After a minute Shelby became aware of Matthew's eyes on her.

She squirmed uncomfortably. "Is my hair on crooked?" she asked finally.

Matthew threw her a playful grin. "No, but at least it's dry," he said.

Shelby swatted at him with her napkin. "Yes, well, as I remember, some klutz dumped me in the lake."

"A pretty klutz," Matthew said smoothly. "Even when she's wet." He patted Shelby's hand. "With a little practice, you'll do just fine."

"A little practice? You mean you're willing to risk it again?"

Matthew pretended to ponder the question. "Well, I might consider it for a price." He leaned over and whispered in her ear, and Shelby giggled as his breath tickled her neck. "How about a kiss for every capsize?"

Shelby shook her head. "Too high a price," she said firmly. "I guess I'll just have to find someone else to practice with. Someone who doesn't charge so much."

Matthew sobered. "Speaking of practice, I thought I saw Pam out on the tennis court tonight." He looked concerned. "But more to the point, Donna was walking in that direction. I'm sure she saw Pam, too."

Shelby raised her eyebrows. "Uh-oh. Well, Pam can't say I didn't warn her. We had a talk tonight in the library," she added in response to Matthew's quizzical look. "But I think the problem may be more serious than a little tennis during library hours."

Matthew wadded up his hamburger wrapper and dropped it into the trash can with a perfect loop shot. "What now?"

Shelby told him what Pam had said about the missing evidence.

"I sure hope she's not thinking of fabricating evidence to support her argument." Matthew folded his arms across his chest. "Donna's pretty sharp. She'll never let Pam get away with it. And I know for a fact that she's watching Pam pretty carefully."

Shelby fished a piece of ice out of her soft drink cup and chewed on it, thinking about Donna. "Oh, I don't think Pam will actually cheat," she said, wishing she hadn't said anything to Matthew about her conversation with Pam. "I really don't think debating means that much to her. She's concentrating on getting ready for her tennis tournament. If she wins, she expects to get a job coaching tennis next year—and a college scholarship the year after that."

Matthew stretched out his long legs and leaned back against the wall, draping his arm comfortably around Shelby's shoulders. "What about you, Shelby? What are you going to do after all this is over? What'll you be doing when you don't have assignments at the library or long lines at the bowling alley to fill up your evenings?"

Shelby turned to him, her heart climbing up into her throat. She'd been putting off thinking about it. But debate camp would be over soon, and she and Matthew would be going in different directions. What *would* she do when she couldn't see him every day, couldn't discuss debate with him, or go sailing? She knew now that her relationship with Tom was over. And there wasn't anyone at school she wanted to date. Did that mean that she'd be alone next year?

"I don't know what I'll do," she responded hesitantly. She tucked one blue-jeaned leg under her on the bench and leaned into the curve of Matthew's arm. "I guess I'll see whether Mom and Dad can use any help in their office or look around for a part-time job—in the library, maybe."

Matthew looked serious. "That wasn't exactly what I meant." He turned so that he could look into her eyes. "I meant—well, are you going back to a boyfriend or anything like that?"

"No, there's nobody back home," Shelby said. "There was a guy I went with for a long time, but we broke up because—" She hesitated. Should she tell Matthew why she and Tom had broken up? "We broke up just before I came to debate camp," she finished hurriedly. There was no point in telling him the whole story.

For a moment there was silence, and then she asked, as casually as she could manage, "What about you? Do you have a special girl back home? Or a half-dozen girls?" She held her breath, waiting for his answer.

Then Matthew reached for her hand. "No, no special girl," he said very quietly, and she had to bend to hear him over the noise of crashing pins. "And no girls, either." He looked down at their tightly joined fingers. "If you haven't guessed by now, Shelby, I don't want this to end when debate camp is over. I want us to go on being. . . ." The sentence hung, unfinished, between them.

"Being friends?" Shelby said finally. She felt

breathless and light-headed, and her hands were icy cold.

"No, more than that," Matthew replied softly. He traced the outline of her cheek with one finger, and his eyes held hers. "A lot more than that. I want you to be my steady girlfriend."

An immense wave of joy flooded through Shelby and left her weak and trembling. A hundred things were on her mind, but she could only say, "Oh, Matthew."

He glanced at her teasingly. "Hey, come on now. Aren't you the one with all the smart talk in debate? The girl who always has to have the last word? What's this 'oh' stuff?"

Shelby swallowed hard, looking up at him. "It means, 'Oh, Matthew, I'm very happy,' " she said breathlessly.

Without caring who was watching, Matthew pulled her against him and kissed her quickly. "Then it's all settled?" he asked huskily. "It won't be easy, living as far apart as we do, but I think we can manage."

Shelby nodded happily. "It's all settled," she whispered. She had never been so happy in her whole life.

Just then Kelly came over to them, a clipboard in his hand. "You two still want to bowl?" he inquired with a wink. Shelby felt her cheeks growing warmer and knew she must be blushing. But for once she didn't care.

The next few days were so busy that Shelby could hardly remember anything but a happy blur. She and Marty won both of their practice debates, one easily, the other "by a hair" as Marty laughingly said afterward.

"But even as close as it was, we were really good," Marty boasted at lunch to Pam and Matthew and Hal, a short, freckled boy who was Pam's new debate partner. They were sitting by the window, at the table where Shelby had met Matthew that first day.

Pam sighed and vigorously attacked her plate of lasagna. "Sure wish we could say the same thing," she muttered fervently with a meaningful glance at Hal.

Hal gave her a friendly grin. "Now, if Donna would only let Pam substitute a tennis match for one of our practice rounds, we'd be in great shape."

Matthew laughed shortly. "What kind of a chance do you think *that* idea has?" he asked.

Pam shook her head. "Maybe by the time the rest of you are ready for the tournament, Donna will decide that Hal and I are as good as we're ever going to get and let us go."

Shelby glanced at Pam. "Did you ever find that piece of evidence you were looking for?"

Pam shrugged and reached for a piece of garlic bread, dropping her eyes. "Let's just say I took care of it. OK?"

Shelby started to say something and then closed her mouth abruptly. Whatever Pam had done, it was *her* business. Shelby didn't want to know about it. She was sorry she had brought it up, especially in front of Matthew.

"Hey, speak of the devil," Hal muttered under his breath. "Here she comes. And it looks like she's headed straight for our table. Watch out!"

Shelby looked up. Donna was striding purposefully toward them, and in a moment she stood beside the table. "Hello," she said, nodding at Matthew and Shelby.

"Would you like to join us?" Matthew asked.

Donna shook her head. She looked down at Pam, and Shelby followed her glance. Shocked, she saw that Pam had turned pale and was staring down at her hands, which were clenched together tightly.

For a second there was silence, and then Donna said, "Pam, I'd like to see you in the squad room right after lunch, please." She turned and walked back across the room while they all stared after her.

"What was that all about?" Hal asked. "What have you done to be summoned into the almighty's royal presence?"

"I—I can't imagine," Pam said carelessly, with a noncommittal shrug. There were two bright spots of color high on her cheeks. "Well, enough of all this foolishness," she said, standing up and squaring her shoulders defiantly. She picked up her tray. "Guess I'd better go see what Her Majesty has in mind." But in spite of Pam's defiant tone, Shelby thought that she looked scared and vulnerable.

Chapter Eleven

Shelby took the stairs two at a time, anxious to change into her shorts and head for the lake with Matthew for an hour's sail before dinner. Brian had kept them a little later than usual, but they'd had a good session, and nobody minded the extra time.

As Shelby opened the door to her room, she gave a surprised gasp. Pam's drawers were all pulled open, and her suitcases and duffel bag were on the bed.

"Pam! What's going on?" Shelby asked, bewildered. "What are you doing?"

Pam regarded her distantly, her face pale and set. "What does it look like I'm doing?" she snapped, stuffing a dirty towel into an already bulging duffel bag. "I'm packing."

"But—but you can't go home! Camp isn't over."

"It's over for me," Pam replied a little more calmly. "I should have gone home when I was assigned to Donna's squad." She paused and took a deep breath. "No, better yet, I shouldn't have come at all. I should have stayed home and worked on my tennis." She stuffed a pair of socks into a corner of her suitcase and slammed it shut decisively. "Anyway, I'm going home. My mom should be here soon to pick me up."

"But what will Donna say?" Shelby asked. "And Hal? He's your debate partner—what will *he* do?"

Pam laughed shortly. "Hal can take care of himself. He's a survivor. And Donna—" She paused, and her glance faltered. "Donna knows all about this."

Suddenly Shelby understood. "Donna knows? You mean—"

"Right. Donna didn't like the way I handled that piece of evidence. She said she thought I—cheated." Suddenly Pam choked on a sob, and she sat down on the edge of the bed, her shoulders heaving.

"Honest, Shelby, I *wasn't* cheating. I *know* I saw that quote somewhere. I even wrote a note to myself to remind me about it. But I clipped the note to the front of the magazine, and then I—I lost the magazine. I just couldn't remember which one it was in. And so I—I invented a reference for it on one of my evidence cards. Donna accused me of fabricating evidence. And now. . . ." She took a deep breath and raised her chin with a calm dignity. "Maybe I've been lazy. And maybe I've taken shortcuts. And maybe I have other priorities. But I'm *not* a cheater. I told Donna I'd rather go home than have her accuse me of that in front of everyone."

Shelby sat down on the bed and put her arm around Pam's shoulders. "Listen, Pam," she said desperately, "we can't just let this happen! Maybe Matthew can talk Donna out of it. Maybe we can get Dr. Lewis to—"

Pam shook her head and smiled wanly. "Thanks, Shelby, but no thanks. I don't want to call anybody's attention to this. And, anyway, I really do need to get home. There just aren't enough hours in the day for debate and tennis, and I can't afford to sacrifice tennis for debate—particularly when I'm not a very good debater."

"Are you sure? Won't you at least let me *try* to do something?" Shelby asked, her eyes filling with tears.

Pam turned to her. "Yes, there is one thing you can do for me," she said fiercely. "I'm going to win the tennis tournament—I *know* it. And I want you to win next week, too, and show everybody what a terrific debater you are—just for me." Then she paused and added thoughtfully, "No, don't do it for me. Do it for *yourself.* You won't feel good about yourself unless you give it everything you have."

Shelby tried to smile. "You're sure giving me a tough assignment."

Pam shook her head hard. "Not a bit, Shelby. You're a winner. The only trouble is that you don't always act like you *know* it." She grabbed Shelby's shoulders with both hands. "You've got to promise me that you'll win—not just for me but for you, too. Promise?"

For a minute, Shelby stared at her, and then she nodded. "I promise," she whispered.

After Pam had gone, the room seemed so empty it almost echoed. Pam had gotten much better about hanging up her clothes and picking up her magazines and papers, but she hadn't been perfect, by any means, and Shelby had grown accustomed to dirty socks hung on the doorknob, T-shirts draped over the mirror, and papers stacked on the desk. Now, with the other bed neatly made with dorm sheets and a blanket and the second closet empty, except for some magazines, she felt a sudden loneliness. She still had some cleaning to do—Pam had asked her to return the magazines to the library and take her evidence file to Hal—but already there was a gap in Shelby's life. There was no doubt about it. She was going to miss Pam—miss her noisy, bouncy exuberance, her single-minded seriousness about tennis. She'd even miss Pam's last-minute efforts to get her assignments done.

"Hey, Shelby. Hey, up there!"

A furtive voice interrupted her thoughts, and Shelby went to the window. Alex was standing at the base of the spruce tree, his hands in his pockets, a look of consternation on his face. "Hey, is it really true?" he asked worriedly. "Did Pam get kicked out for cheating?"

Shelby shook her head. "No, that's not the way it was at all," she said firmly. "Pam just decided that it would be better for her to spend her time on tennis. And that's all there is to it."

A look of relief flooded Alex's face. "Hey, that's great," he said enthusiastically. "I mean, I'll miss her and all that—she was lots of fun. But I'd really hate to think that she got kicked out."

"Well, she didn't," Shelby said and shut the window.

Matthew reacted stoically to Shelby's news. "It was only a matter of time," he said as they raised the sail on the Sunfish and got ready to push it into the water. "Donna sets high standards, and Pam just couldn't seem to understand that."

"Pam *did* understand," Shelby insisted, fastening the halyard to the mast. "She has high expectations of herself, too. It's just that her priorities are different." She sighed. "This whole thing is like an argument where there's no clear right or wrong. There are just—just *two* sides."

"Except that Pam cheated," Matthew reminded her. He handed her the life jackets to be stowed in the stern.

Shelby straightened up and looked at him intently. "She made up a reference, and that was wrong. But I believe that she saw that piece of evidence. Somewhere. She was just so—so poorly organized that she couldn't remember where she saw it."

"Well, in Donna's mind it's the same thing," Matthew observed dryly. He gave her hand a quick squeeze. "Now come on, it's going to be too dark for sailing if we don't get started."

But Shelby couldn't get Pam out of her mind—the half-empty room was a sharp reminder of her absence. But she knew she had to concentrate on her own debating. It paid off; the next day she and Marty won their third practice round.

"Good job, kids," Brian said after the debate was over and the squad had critiqued their performances. "You two are getting pretty good. I think both of you have a real chance in the tournament next week."

"It would be great if we could stay together," Marty said, glancing at Shelby. "I'd have a lot better chance if Shelby and I were teamed."

Shelby smiled happily. She felt she really *had* improved—if only because she was losing her fear of speaking in front of a group. The words came so much more easily now, and she had achieved a fluidity that improved her speaking and even made her gestures look more natural. "Thanks, Marty," she said.

"Well, it's the truth," Marty persisted. "Whoever gets you as a partner will be really lucky." He turned to Brian. "When will the teams be announced?"

"Dr. Lewis said they'd be posted on the bulletin board in the dorm lounge where Kelly is holding another 'fun-and-frivolity' hour tonight," Brian said. "You can check the list there. That includes the announcement of the two people who have been chosen for the pair debating." He gave Shelby a brief, questioning glance she couldn't decipher. "It looks like a terrific tournament."

Everybody attended Kelly's social hours to

unwind with soft drinks, potato chips, and popcorn. But that night no one was at the snack table. Everyone was clustered around the bulletin board, looking at the tournament team assignments.

"Let's go look," Shelby urged as she and Matthew walked into the room. Ever since the strange glance Brian had given her earlier in the afternoon, she had wondered about her assignment. And Matthew hadn't given her a hint, even though she had the strong feeling that he knew what the assignments were.

Matthew took her arm and steered her toward the snack table. "There's plenty of time. Look at that mob. We couldn't even get close to the bulletin board." He popped the top on a can of ginger ale and handed her the drink.

"But aren't you curious?" Shelby asked. "After all, you're going to be in the tournament, too." She reached for a handful of popcorn. "Or maybe you already know your teammate."

Before Matthew could respond, Marty bounded across the room, beaming. "Well, I must say that you two superstars are sure taking it calmly." He enveloped Shelby in a friendly bear hug. "Let me be the first to congratulate you."

Shelby looked at him blankly. "Superstars?" she asked. "What are you talking about?"

"Why, I'm talking about the tournament assignments, of course. What else would I be talking about?" Marty looked at her, then swiveled to stare at Matthew. "You mean she doesn't know?"

"Know *what*?" Shelby demanded impatiently. Why was Matthew looking so mysterious? And what was Marty babbling about? She started toward the bulletin board, but Matthew pulled her back.

Marty looked at her in surprise for a moment, and then he whistled. "Oops, sorry, Shelby. I thought you knew about the assignments. About the paired debate."

Shelby stared first at Marty and then at Matthew, a horrible suspicion forming in her mind. "The paired debate?" she whispered.

Matthew grinned broadly and clinked his ginger ale can against hers in a toast. "Here's to us, Shelby. Dr. Lewis chose us to compete against each other in the paired debate. Congratulations!"

Shelby stared at him, feeling herself turning cold, then hot, then cold again. "The paired debate?" she whispered again. "Oh, no!"

Marty gave her a puzzled look and then shook his head. "Hey, Shelby, that's not the way you're supposed to react." He grabbed her and danced her around in a victory jig. "You're supposed to be *happy*. This assignment goes to the best debaters, not the worst! Come on, smile!"

But when Marty had released her, Shelby could only stare at them, limp and dumbfounded. It couldn't be happening again, it couldn't be possible! She looked imploringly at Matthew. "Can't you *do* something?" she pleaded. "Can't you ask Dr. Lewis to choose somebody else?" She tried to suppress the panic in her voice.

Matthew frowned. "I don't understand, Shelby. I thought you'd be pleased. Usually it's only the second-year debaters who get assigned to pair debating. It's a real honor—"

Shelby shook her head frantically. "I know. But I *can't*, Matthew. You don't understand. I can't." She looked up at him, but it was Tom's face she saw, taut and angry. "Please, can't we do something to change the assignment?"

Matthew smiled, but there was no smile in his eyes. "I'm afraid not. It's always a tough job to get everybody placed, and once the assignments are set, Dr. Lewis won't make any exceptions." He looked down at his watch. "We have a half hour until curfew. Come on, Shelby, let's get out of here. You're going to tell me what this is all about."

The moon glinted brightly on the water as

they sat in silence on the footbridge, in the shadow of the willow tree. All Shelby could hear was the wind in the branches and the thump of her heart in her throat. What could she say to Matthew? She couldn't tell him about Tom—could she? But how else could she explain her reluctance to oppose him in the debate?

"Well?" Matthew demanded. "Are you going to tell me what's going on?" He reached for Shelby's hand, and his voice was softer. "Whatever it is, it can't make any difference to *us*, Shelby."

Shelby closed her eyes and tried again. "Matthew, I want to get the pairing changed," she pleaded. "You don't understand—"

"Yes, that much is obvious," Matthew interrupted. He pulled her closer to him, tucking her hand under his arm, and his warmth began to flow comfortingly through her. "I don't understand. There must be some reason."

Shelby drew a slow breath. "I just don't think it's a good idea for the two of us to debate each other," she said evasively. Even to her ears, the words sounded weak and dishonest.

Matthew said softly, "Are you afraid to lose, Shelby? Are you afraid that might make a difference in the way you feel about me?"

Shelby stared at him. "Is that what you think?" she asked. She tried to swallow the nervous giggle that rose in her throat. "That I'm afraid to *lose*?" She shook her head violently. She would have to tell him. "The truth is, Matthew," she whispered, "that I'm afraid to *win*."

When she had finished telling him about Tom, Matthew was silent for a long time, so long that Shelby began to wonder whether he had heard. Then he turned and put both hands on her shoulders. She couldn't read his eyes in the darkness, but the lines around his mouth were tender.

"I think I understand how rough it must have been for you, Shelby," he said sincerely. "But you can't judge me by the way Tom acted. I'm a different person." He paused. "And I'm not afraid. I think Tom was."

"Afraid?"

"It's just human nature to like things the way they are, Shelby. You and Tom were together a long time, and your relationship must have seemed very safe and comfortable and predictable to him. When you started to change, all that was threatened." He stopped and thought for a minute. "Maybe it wasn't your winning that threatened him so much as the change itself."

He picked up her hand and traced the outline of her fingers. "I'm not afraid. Change is part of human nature, too. It's not easy, but very few worthwhile things are. The trick is for two people to change at the same pace, so that one doesn't get left behind." He looked up, and Shelby could see the ghost of a smile at the corners of his lips. "Some people manage it, Shelby. I think *we* can." His emphasis on "we" suddenly made what he said very personal.

"I'm still afraid, Matthew," she whispered. "I understand what you're saying, but somehow. . . ." She swallowed hard. There was a tight, cold knot inside her, and even the warmth in Matthew's words couldn't dissolve it. She kept hearing the echo of Tom's words: *"A guy can't go out with a girl who upstages him all the time."*

"Just trust me, Shelby," Matthew insisted softly. "Win or lose, I want us to be together."

The cold inside her lingered even after Matthew's good night kiss. Shelby wanted to believe Matthew when he said he wanted them to stay together no matter what happened. But as she lay in bed that night trying to fall asleep, she wasn't comforted.

Chapter Twelve

The next morning after a long, sleepless night, Shelby went to see Dr. Lewis in her office in the library.

"Congratulations, Shelby." Dr. Lewis stood and held out her hand, smiling happily. Her desk was cluttered with papers, and on the table behind the desk stood various trophies that Shelby guessed had been won in previous years by the college debating teams. "It isn't often that we have a first-year debater who's good enough to handle pair debating. We're all looking forward to an exciting debate. Now, what can I do for you?"

"I wonder—" Shelby said hesitantly and then straightened her shoulders. Dr. Lewis's congratulations made it harder, but she had to try. "I wonder if it's possible to change the pair-debating assignment," she said as calmly as she could. Remembering her unsuccessful efforts to convince Matthew, she had come prepared with what she hoped was a plausible-sounding reason. "I'd really rather work on a team than debate one-on-one." She tried to put more enthusiasm into her voice, adding in a rush, "A team is so much more satisfying because you get to work closely with somebody else."

"Are you sure there's not another reason, my dear?" Dr. Lewis asked gravely. She frowned. "You've been doing team debating for a long while now, and the challenge of individual debating is an important step for you. And I know you've done it successfully before."

Shelby looked down. How could she tell Dr. Lewis that she was afraid that winning the debate might mean losing Matthew, just as she had lost Tom? That the recollection of Tom's rejection was even stronger and more compelling than Matthew's calm reassurances. "No, there's no other reason," she answered.

"Well, then, let's just leave things as they stand," Dr. Lewis said brightly. She put her hand on Shelby's shoulder and smiled proudly. "I know you'll do a good job, Shelby. It will be quite a challenge for you to go up against Matthew since he's had more experience. But it's a challenge you're up to. Everything will turn out all right—you'll see."

I wish I could believe that, Shelby thought as she left the office.

But if it had been hard to deal with Dr. Lewis's confident assertions, it was also difficult to accept her friends' congratulations. That afternoon at lunch Laura charged up to her as she stood by the milk dispenser. "Congratulations, Shel. You two will be terrific opponents."

"Thanks, I think," Shelby mumbled as she set her glass on her tray. Belatedly, she looked up and attempted a small smile. "Who are you teamed with?"

"Marty and I are working together," Laura told her exuberantly. "Aren't I lucky? I hear that he was really good in the practice rounds."

Shelby glanced at Laura enviously. If she could only have been teamed with Marty, everything would have been so much simpler. "Yes, you're really lucky," she said. "The two of you will make a good team."

On the surface nothing seemed to change between Shelby and Matthew. Since neither of them had to spend any time in team practice, they had a few more hours for jogging, horseback riding, and sailing. Shelby became proficient enough with the sailboat to manage a series of tacks across the lake without capsizing, and even though she'd never been much of a rider, she could now handle her horse with much greater skill. If only it hadn't been for the debate, she thought sadly, these days would have been wonderful—days to remember always.

Although nothing appeared to be different, Shelby felt a terrible strain, a kind of anxious anticipation. She watched Matthew for signs that he felt the same tension, but he was as considerate as always, and she finally concluded that the anxiety was mostly inside her.

And to make matters even worse, a new thought had come to her one afternoon as she and Matthew staged an impromptu horse race across the meadow. "Beat you to the pine tree over there," Matthew had yelled at her, and she kicked her bay gelding hard in the flanks and took off. It was a dead heat all the way, but in the last few seconds Matthew's horse seemed to flag, and Shelby's won by a nose. But as she turned her horse back toward him, she caught a fleeting glimpse of a grin.

"Did you throw the race?" she demanded. "Did you pull back?"

"Now, whatever gave you that idea?" Matthew replied, innocence written all over his face. He leaned forward and rubbed his horse between the ears. "I guess this old guy just doesn't have it in him anymore," he added. "I hope I didn't make him lame by pushing him too hard."

But the race had given her an idea. And as the days went on, it began to seem more and more attractive. In the weeks after she and Tom had broken up, she had thought longingly of how different it would have been if she had lost the debate. Well, losing was under *her* control, wasn't it? Nobody could ever be sure of winning, but *anybody* could be sure of losing. All she had to do was stumble a little in her presentation or omit an important piece of evidence or forget to answer a point. It would be easy to lose, and no one would even know what had happened—no one but her.

It was difficult for Shelby to settle down to work. One evening she sat down at her desk to go over her notes, but she kept remembering the way Tom behaved after she had won the debate. In spite of what Matthew had said, there was a chance that if she won, he'd feel the same way.

Finally she forced herself to shut off her thoughts. Trying halfheartedly to anticipate how Matthew would approach the argument, she revised her plan of attack. There was a big gap in her argument—and then she remembered the evidence that Pam had been searching for. *That* was what she needed, she told herself. But Pam hadn't been able to locate it—assuming it actually existed. Even though her argument lacked that final clincher, she'd just have to be satisfied with what she already had.

On the day before the debate Shelby remembered that she had promised to return Pam's books to the library. Pam had stacked some of them beside the door, but there were the others in the closet and a few still scattered under Pam's bed, and it took Shelby a few minutes to gather them all.

She was stacking the magazines when she discovered it. For an instant she didn't recognize what she was holding. It was a magazine with a note on yellow paper clipped to it. "Good evidence on jobs!" the note said, and when Shelby opened the magazine and began to read the passages Pam had marked, her heart jumped a beat. This was the evidence that Pam had been looking for! The evidence she hadn't been able to find because it was—of all places—under her *bed*!

A hundred thoughts flew through Shelby's mind. The evidence was important, all right, probably the most important piece of evidence in the entire argument. It practically clinched her most significant point. If she used it, she could win. Without it, Matthew's argument would be stronger, and her problem would be solved.

But that wasn't fair to Pam, Shelby thought. She sat down cross-legged on her bed and tried to think. For Pam's sake, she would have to show the magazine to Donna, and Donna would have to admit that Pam hadn't cheated. But if she showed it to Donna, she'd have to use the evidence in her argument. And she'd also have to let Matthew know about it, so he could decide how to argue against it. She looked down at Pam's scrawled note and sighed, knowing what she had to do.

Donna was in the squad room all alone, cleaning off the shelves. She looked up and smiled when she saw Shelby, and Shelby was surprised at how relaxed she looked, now that the camp was nearly over. "Hello, Shelby," she said. There was something that sounded like genuine welcome in her voice. "I haven't had a chance yet to tell you how glad I am that they chose you for the pair debating. You might not win, but you'll give Matthew a real challenge."

"It sounds as though you've already decided the outcome," Shelby said a little defensively.

Donna went back to her work. "Matthew has had more experience," she said quietly.

Shelby stood straighter. "Maybe so, but I've learned a lot in the last couple of weeks."

Donna faced her, her gaze steady and direct. "Do you think you've learned enough to win?"

"Yes." The word came out before Shelby realized what she had said, and surprised, she added, a little more tentatively, "At least I think I have." Suddenly Pam's words echoed through her head. *"You can win,"* Pam had insisted. And thinking back on everything she had learned in the last month, she knew she had all the skills to win.

Donna looked at her with surprised approval. "Yes, I think you have, too," she said, nodding. "But you're not going to win unless you *want* to, Shelby. Unless you decide that winning is important to you and to everyone who believes in you—including Matthew. Once you decide to live up to that challenge, you can win." She turned back to the shelf and began to rearrange a stack of books. "Of course, if you decide that other things are more important," she added offhandedly, "you'll let Matthew beat you. It's just a matter of getting your priorities straight."

Shelby was quiet for a moment. Then she asked, "Is that what you said to Pam?"

"Something like that. Pam could have been a good debater if she'd wanted to work for it. But she really wanted to work for something else, and it was a waste of her time to be here." She paused and looked at Shelby closely. "Pam went home because *she* decided to, Shelby. It was the right decision."

Shelby took a deep breath and held out the magazine, Pam's scrawled note still clipped to the cover. "I wanted you to know that Pam didn't cheat—she just couldn't remember where she'd seen the evidence she was looking for."

Donna flicked a glance at the magazine, and Shelby thought she saw a hint of a smile. "I know."

"But when she couldn't find the reference, you accused her of cheating!" Shelby burst out. "You accused her of fabricating evidence."

Donna stepped closer and put her hand on Shelby's shoulder. "No, I accused Pam of disappointing herself by taking shortcuts, like making up a reference to something she thought she'd read but couldn't really remember. I accused her of not living up to her potential. I told her to decide what her real priorities were. But I didn't accuse her of cheating."

"But Pam said. . . ." Suddenly Shelby began to understand.

"That's OK," Donna said sympathetically. "Maybe it was easier for Pam to explain what happened that way. Now, maybe you should call Pam and tell her about finding the magazine," she suggested briskly, squeezing Shelby's shoulder. "You'll also want to share the evidence with Matthew so both of you can use it in your arguments."

Shelby dropped her eyes. Now she was stuck—she'd have to use the evidence, whether she wanted to or not. She turned toward the door.

"Wait, Shelby," Donna said quickly. "You're going to do a great job in the debate if you relax and stop worrying about winning or losing. Just do a job you can be proud of. I'm sure that's what Pam would want you to do. OK?"

"OK," she said quietly. "I will. And thanks. Thanks for everything."

Matthew gave a long, low whistle as he leafed through the pages of the magazine that Shelby showed him in the library that evening. "Well, I guess I'd better make some quick revisions in what I was planning to say tomorrow," he said thoughtfully. He turned back to the front cover and Pam's note. "So she really was on to something after all."

"I've already talked to Donna," Shelby said quietly. "And I called Pam this afternoon. She said to tell everybody that her backhand is better than ever and she's planning on winning next week."

Matthew grinned. "Same old Pam, huh?"

He looked at her sideways. "Well, maybe not *exactly* the same Pam—or at least not the way I thought about her."

Shelby stood up. "Tomorrow's a big day, and my parents are going to be here early. I think I'll go back to my room and look over my notes."

"My parents will be here, too. I'd like it if you could meet them."

Shelby frowned uncertainly. "Maybe we'd better wait until after the debate and see how we feel then."

Matthew looked at her intently. "Whatever happens in the debate tomorrow, Shelby, it's not going to change the way I feel about you."

"I know, Matthew," she said steadily. "And I'm not going to worry about winning—or losing. I'm just going to do my best."

Matthew broke into a wide grin and hugged her, hard. "That's what I want to hear. And that goes for both of us."

Chapter Thirteen

Shelby had been up very early, organizing the notes that she would take to the auditorium. Her clothes were already packed, too, so all she had to do after the debate was put her suitcases in her parents' car and drive home. *Home.* At home there wouldn't be any Matthew, and no more lovely, lingering afternoons beside the lake or in the fragrant woods. After that day things would be different. But exactly how, she couldn't be sure, and the uncertainty was unnerving. Forcing herself to concentrate, Shelby busied herself reviewing her notes and dressing.

Shelby had thought for a long time about what she would wear for the debate and finally settled on a gray skirt and her favorite gray-and-pink plaid roll-sleeve blouse. The outfit was dressy, especially with her gold beads, yet casual enough to be comfortable. Her cheeks shone with a healthy, rosy glow from the time spent swimming and horseback riding with Matthew. Looking in the mirror, Shelby was pleased with what she saw. Maybe she didn't have Holly's blond, baby-doll daintiness, but the mirror told her that she looked prettier than she ever had.

Although the tournament had begun the day before, most people had come to see the championship rounds and the paired debating, which were scheduled the second day. Shelby had watched part of the championship debates, then gone back to her room to go over her notes one last time.

When she returned to the auditorium, Dr. Lewis and Matthew were already waiting backstage. "Both of you will sit at that table," Dr. Lewis said, pointing toward a long empty table in the middle of the stage. "The podium has a microphone. I've already tested it so we know it's working." She smiled at Shelby. "Don't let it make you nervous."

Shelby nodded numbly. She wasn't really nervous, although her hands were cold and clammy and there was a tight, hard knot in her stomach. She looked quickly at Matthew, standing straight and tall in his dark gray suit. He wore a vest and a blue- and gray-striped tie that made his eyes seem even bluer.

Shelby gulped. She had always known Matthew was handsome, but that day, dressed the way he was, he had a dignity and maturity that made Tom seem like a little boy beside him. But the suit also made him seem— different, somehow. More distant, less approachable, a stranger. This calm, remote young man didn't seem like the Matthew who had held her tightly beside the lake in the silver moonlight. The Matthew who had kissed her in the bowling alley and asked her to be his girlfriend. She shut her eyes against the recollection. No, looking at Matthew standing so tall and serious beside Dr. Lewis, she couldn't believe that he was the same person.

"OK, it's time," Dr. Lewis whispered. "I'm going to announce the winners of the tournament, and then we'll get started. Good luck, both of you."

The small auditorium was crowded with debaters and their parents and friends. After a month of nothing but T-shirts and shorts and blue jeans, it was strange to see everyone all dressed up. The boys wore suits and sports jackets and ties, their hair carefully slicked down. The girls were dressed in pretty pastel dresses, and some of them wore heels and makeup.

As Dr. Lewis stood up to announce the

winners, everyone listened with eager anticipation.

"In the championship bracket, our final winners are Laura Lacy and Marty Thomas," she said, and there was a loud cheer from the debaters as Laura and Marty proudly got up from their places in the audience to accept their trophy. Standing self-consciously and a little stiffly next to Matthew backstage, Shelby admired the easy, natural way Laura accepted Dr. Lewis's words of praise. "No doubt about it, she's going to be class president next year," Matthew whispered to Shelby, and Shelby nodded a little enviously. Laura had what it took to succeed, and it didn't seem to bother her at all.

After the list of winners in both the consolation and the championship brackets had been announced, Dr. Lewis continued, "And now we will have the pair debate, the individual event that all of us look forward to each year. In this event two of our very best debaters compete against each other. Like all debaters, they will be judged not only on their arguments but on their presentations and their poise. This year, we have selected two very fine debaters, Matthew Benson and Shelby Scott." As Shelby and Matthew walked out onto the stage, there was applause. They both sat down at the table. "Matthew is a second-year debater who has been working at the camp as a squad assistant," Dr. Lewis went on. "Shelby is a first-year debater who won the pair debate event in her high school last spring."

Dr. Lewis turned to the three judges sitting on the front row. "Are the judges ready?" Then she turned to Shelby and Matthew. "If the debaters are ready, we'll begin. Shelby will have ten minutes to make her argument. Matthew will follow with a fifteen-minute rebuttal. Shelby will then conclude with a five-minute summary. Shelby, are you ready?"

Shelby nodded and stood up, and then she glanced hesitantly at Matthew. He was looking up, smiling expectantly. And then behind the table, where the audience couldn't see him, he raised his hand, thumb up. "Go get 'em, Shelby," he whispered. And suddenly everything seemed right to Shelby, and she smiled in return. "Thanks. You, too," she whispered back.

As she stood at the podium, the auditorium lights went dim, and Shelby couldn't see beyond the second or third row. But she knew that her parents and Roger and Mr. Lawsen were out there somewhere, expecting her to do a good job. And Matthew, too, expected her to do her best, regardless of the outcome. She looked up into the blinding spotlight and smiled. Suddenly she felt a new confidence, and as she looked down at her notes and remembered the arguments she was going to present, she knew that she would do a good job.

"Ladies and gentlemen," she began confidently, "today I am going to tell you why the federal government should take over the air travel industry. After I have made my arguments, my opponent, Matthew Benson, will tell you why the airlines should be left to struggle alone to solve the problems of mass air transportation. Like most arguments, there are good points on both sides, and I know that my opponent will present strong and convincing reasons for his case. But I believe firmly that in this argument, there is only one final, inevitable answer. I am confident that when all of the arguments are presented, you will agree with my conclusion."

When she sat down at the table ten minutes later, Shelby felt a deep satisfaction. She knew she had made the strongest opening argument she could make. She hadn't left anything out or overstated any of her points. And she had spoken better than ever before, with a brand-new self-assurance that gave a special credibility to her arguments.

Matthew recognized it, too. "Good job," he

whispered as he stood up to go to the podium. "You sure make a tough case. Now let's see what you have to say to *this*."

For the next fifteen minutes Shelby jotted down notes while Matthew spoke, presenting his case and attacking hers. Matthew argued extremely well, and his deep, expressive voice often rose passionately as he made his points. Several times he tapped the podium emphatically as he pointed out the weaknesses of Shelby's argument and developed his own counterpoints. Once he turned to speak directly to her. "My opponent, Shelby Scott, makes an excellent point when she says that a government takeover would stabilize the employment situation for most employees. But I doubt whether she has considered the opposite side of this argument. If the airlines are nationalized, will workers be able to strike to achieve higher wages and better working conditions? No, of course not. They will have to depend on the government to improve their working situation."

Matthew's arguments were easy to follow because they were so clear and because his presentation was so well-organized. But when Shelby got up to begin her five-minute rebuttal, she knew that she could successfully counter every single point he had made. She glanced down at the judges. One of them, leaning forward intently, started his stopwatch and signaled that he had started timing. With confidence, Shelby smiled and launched into her summary.

When she was finished, the audience broke into loud applause. But as Shelby took her seat, she couldn't bear to look at Matthew. She hadn't pulled any punches in her argument. She'd been fair, but tough. And she didn't know how he was going to respond. He'd said he wanted her to be a winner, but she couldn't be sure he had really meant it. She took a deep breath as Dr. Lewis went to the microphone.

"We've seen two very fine debaters at work, and both of them have done a superb job. Now, are the judges ready with their evaluation?" She went to the edge of the stage, took a sheet from one of the judges, and scanned it quickly while Shelby waited breathlessly, her heart pounding. For the first time since it was over, she glanced sideways at Matthew. Her heart sank. He looked so serious, so intent. She could see how much he wanted to win.

"Ladies and gentlemen," Dr. Lewis said, "I am proud to announce that this year's debate has been won by our first-year debater, Shelby Scott. Shelby, will you please come and accept your trophy?"

Flushed with pride and happiness, Shelby stood, but she didn't go immediately to the podium. Instead, she looked down at Matthew. How would he respond? "Matthew?" she whispered uncertainly.

For a very brief instant she could read the disappointment in his blue eyes. And then he stood up, with a wide grin on his face, and held out both hands. "Congratulations, Shelby," he said. He stepped forward and gave her a quick, hard hug. "You did a terrific job. I'm *so* proud of you."

"Do you mean that?" Shelby asked, searching his eyes. And when he nodded, Shelby was certain. "But just wait until next time," he cautioned. "Next time I'll know what to expect, and I'll be ready. You haven't had the last word yet. Now, get up there and get your trophy before Dr. Lewis decides to give it to the runner-up."

Happily Shelby stepped forward to the podium to accept the large golden trophy that Dr. Lewis was holding. "Congratulations, Shelby," Dr. Lewis said as she shook Shelby's hand. "The judges found your presentation to be very persuasive, and they especially commented on the confidence and poise with which you presented your arguments. Now, would you like to say anything?"

Shelby stepped forward to the microphone, suddenly sure of what she wanted to say. "Yes, I'd like to thank my mother and father and my debate coach, Mr. Lawsen, for their confidence in me. And I would especially like to thank my friend Matthew Benson for helping me to understand that it's really OK to win. Without his encouragement, it would have been awfully easy to lose."

She turned back to her seat, with the applause ringing in her ears. Off in the wings, she could see a crowd of people gathered to congratulate her—her parents and Roger and Mr. Lawsen, and Donna, Brian, Laura, and Marty, too. But for an instant Matthew's eyes found hers, and as he held out his hand, she felt a deep and rich happiness. They couldn't know what was ahead, but she knew that whatever happened, they could meet it together.

A LETTER TO THE READER

Dear Friend,

Ever since I created the series, SWEET VALLEY HIGH, I've been thinking about a love trilogy, a miniseries revolving around one very special girl, a character similar in some ways to Jessica Wakefield, but even more devastating—more beautiful, more charming, and much more devious.

Her name is Caitlin Ryan, and with her long black hair, her magnificent blue eyes and ivory complexion, she's the most popular girl at the exclusive boarding school she attends in Virginia. On the surface her life seems perfect. She has it all: great wealth, talent, intelligence, and the dazzle to charm every boy in the school. But deep inside there's a secret need that haunts her life.

Caitlin's mother died in childbirth, and her father abandoned her immediately after she was born. At least that's the lie she has been told by her enormously rich grandmother, the cold and powerful matriarch who has raised Caitlin and given her everything money can buy. But not love.

Caitlin dances from boy to boy, never staying long, often breaking hearts, yet she's so sparkling and delightful that everyone forgives her. No one can resist her.

No one that is, but Jed Michaels. He's the new boy in school—tall, wonderfully handsome, and very, very nice. And Caitlin means to have him.

But somehow the old tricks don't work; she can't

seem to manipulate him. Impossible! There has never been anyone that the beautiful and terrible Caitlin couldn't have. And now she wants Jed Michaels—no matter who gets hurt or what she has to do to get him.

So many of you follow my SWEET VALLEY HIGH series that I know you'll find it fascinating to read what happens when love comes into the life of this spoiled and selfish beauty—the indomitable Caitlin Ryan.

Thanks for being there, and keep reading,

Francine Pascal

A special preview of the exciting
opening chapter of the first book
in the fabulous new trilogy:

CAITLIN

BOOK ONE

LOVING

---

by Francine Pascal,
creator of the best-selling
SWEET VALLEY HIGH series

"That's not a bad idea, Tenny," Caitlin said as she reached for a book from her locker. "Actually, it's pretty good."

"You really like it?" Tenny Sears hung on every word the beautiful Caitlin Ryan said. It was the petite freshman's dream to be accepted into the elite group the tall, dark-haired junior led at Highgate Academy. She was ready to do anything to belong.

Caitlin looked around and noticed the group of five girls who had begun to walk their way, and she lowered her voice conspiratorially. "Let me think it over, and I'll get back to you later. Meanwhile let's just keep it between us, okay?"

"Absolutely." Tenny struggled to keep her excitement down to a whisper. The most important girl in the whole school liked her idea. "Cross my heart," she promised. "I won't breathe a word to anyone."

Tenny would have loved to continue the conversation, but at just that moment Caitlin remembered she'd left her gold pen in French class. Tenny was only too happy to race to fetch it.

The minute the younger girl was out of sight, Caitlin gathered the other girls around her.

"Hey, you guys, I just had a great idea for this year's benefit night. Want to hear it?"

Of course they wanted to hear what she had to say about the benefit, the profits of which would go to the scholarship fund for miners' children. Everyone was always interested in anything Caitlin Ryan had to say. She waited until all eyes were on her, then hesitated for an instant, increasing the dramatic impact of her words.

"How about a male beauty contest?"

"A what?" Morgan Conway exclaimed.

"A male beauty contest," Caitlin answered, completely unruffled. "With all the guys dressing up in crazy outfits. It'd be a sellout!"

Most of the girls looked at Caitlin as if she'd suddenly gone crazy, but Dorothy Raite, a sleek, blond newcomer to Highgate, stepped closer to Caitlin's locker. "I think it's a great idea!"

"Thanks, Dorothy," Caitlin said, smiling modestly.

"I don't know." Morgan was doubtful. "How are you going to get the guys to go along with this? I can't quite picture Roger Wake parading around on stage in a swimsuit."

"He'll be the first contestant to sign up when I get done talking to him." Caitlin's tone was slyly smug.

"And all the other guys?"

"They'll follow along." Caitlin placed the last of her books in her knapsack, zipped it shut, then gracefully slung it over her shoulder. "Everybody who's anybody in this school will just shrivel up and die if they can't be part of it. Believe me, I wouldn't let the student council down. After all, I've got my new presidency to live up to."

Morgan frowned. "I suppose." She took a chocolate bar out of her brown leather shoulder bag and began to unwrap it.

Just at that moment, Tenny came back, empty-handed and full of apologies. "Sorry, Caitlin, I asked all over, but nobody's seen it."

"That's okay. I think I left it in my room, anyway."

"Did you lose something?" Kim Verdi asked, but Caitlin dismissed the subject, saying it wasn't important.

For an instant Tenny was confused until Dorothy Raite asked her if she'd heard Caitlin's fabulous new idea for a male beauty contest. Then everything fell into place. Caitlin had sent her away in order to take credit for the idea.

It didn't even take three seconds for Tenny to make up her mind about what to do. "Sounds terrific," she said. Tenny Sears was determined to belong to this group, no matter what.

Dorothy leaned over and whispered to Caitlin. "Speaking of beauties, look who's walking over here."

Casually Caitlin glanced up at the approaching Highgate soccer star. Roger Wake's handsome face broke into a smile when he saw her. Caitlin knew he was interested in her, and up until then she'd offhandedly played with that interest—when she was in the mood.

"And look who's with him!" Dorothy's elbow nearly poked a hole in Caitlin's ribs. "Jed Michaels. Oh, my God, I've been absolutely dying to meet this guy."

Caitlin nodded, her eyes narrowing. She'd been anxious to meet Jed, too, but she didn't tell Dorothy that. Ever since his arrival as a transfer student at Highgate, Caitlin had been studying him, waiting for precisely the right moment to be introduced and to make an unforgettable impression on him. It seemed that the opportunity had just been handed to her.

"Hey, Caitlin. How're you doing?" Roger called out, completely ignoring the other girls in the group.

"Great, Roger. How about you?" Caitlin's smile couldn't have been wider. "Thought you'd be on the soccer field by now."

"I'm on my way. The coach pushed back practice half an hour today, anyway. Speaking of which, I don't remember seeing you at the last scrimmage." There was a hint of teasing in his voice.

Caitlin looked puzzled and touched her fingertips to her lips. "I was there, I'm sure—"

"We were late, Caitlin, remember?" Tenny spoke up eagerly. "I was with you at drama club, and it ran over."

"Now, how could I have forgotten? You see,

Roger"—Caitlin sent him a sly, laughing look—"we never let the team down. Jenny should know—she's one of your biggest fans."

"Tenny," the girl corrected meekly. But she was glowing from having been singled out for attention by Caitlin.

"Oh, right, Tenny. Sorry, but I'm really bad with names sometimes." Caitlin smiled at the girl with seeming sincerity, but her attention returned quickly to the two boys standing nearby.

"Caitlin," Dorothy burst in, "do you want to tell him—"

"Shhh," Caitlin put her finger to her lips. "Not yet. We haven't made all our plans."

"Tell me what?" Roger asked eagerly.

"Oh, just a little idea we have for the council fund-raiser, but it's too soon to talk about it."

"Come on." Roger was becoming intrigued. "You're not being fair, Caitlin."

She paused. "Well, since you're our star soccer player, I can tell you it's going to be the hottest happening at Highgate this fall."

"Oh, yeah? What, a party?"

"No."

"A concert?"

She shook her head, her black-lashed, blue eyes twinkling. "I'm not going to stand here and play Twenty Questions with you, Roger. But when we decide to make our plans public, you'll be the first to know. I promise."

"Guess I'll have to settle for that."

"Anyway, Roger, I promise not to let any of this other stuff interfere with my supporting the team from now on."

At her look, Roger seemed ready to melt into his Nikes.

Just at that moment Jed Michaels stepped forward. It was a casual move on his part, as though he were just leaning in a little more closely to hear the conversation. His gaze rested on Caitlin.

Although she'd deliberately given the impression of being impervious to Jed, Caitlin was acutely aware of every move he made. She'd studied him enough from a distance to know that she liked what she saw.

Six feet tall, with broad shoulders and a trim body used to exercise, Jed Michaels was the type of boy made for a girl like Caitlin. He had wavy, light brown hair, ruggedly even features, and an endearing, crooked smile. Dressed casually in a striped cotton shirt, tight cords, and western boots, Jed didn't look like the typical preppy Highgate student, and Caitlin had the feeling it was a deliberate choice. He looked like his own person.

Caitlin had been impressed before, but now that she saw him close at hand, she felt electrified. For that brief instant when his incredible green eyes had looked directly into hers, she'd felt a tingle go up her spine.

Suddenly realizing the need for an introduction, Roger put his hand on Jed's shoulder. "By the way, do you girls know Jed Michaels? He just transferred here from Montana. We've already got him signed up for the soccer team."

Immediately the girls called out a chorus of enthusiastic greetings, which Jed acknowledged with a friendly smile and a nod of his head. "Nice to meet you." Dorothy's call had been the loudest, and Jed's gaze went toward the pretty blonde.

Dorothy smiled at him warmly, and Jed grinned back. But before another word could be spoken, Caitlin riveted Jed with her most magnetic look.

"I've seen you in the halls, Jed, and hoped you'd been made welcome." The intense fire of her deep blue eyes emphasized her words.

He looked from Dorothy to Caitlin. "Sure have."

"And how do you like Highgate?" Caitlin pressed on quickly, keeping the attention on herself.

"So far, so good." His voice was deep and soft and just slightly tinged with a western drawl.

"I'm glad." The enticing smile never left Caitlin's lips. "What school did you transfer from?"

"A small one back in Montana. You wouldn't have heard of it."

"Way out in cattle country?"

His eyes glimmered. "You've been to Montana?"

"Once. Years ago with my grandmother. It's really beautiful. All those mountains . . ."

"Yeah. Our ranch borders the Rockies."

"Ranch, huh? I'll bet you ride, then."

"Before I could walk."

"Then you'll have to try the riding here—eastern style. It's really fantastic! We're known for our hunt country in this part of Virginia."

"I'd like to try it."

"Come out with me sometime, and I'll show you the trails. I ride almost every afternoon." Caitlin drew her fingers through her long, black hair, pulling it away from her face in a way she knew was becoming, yet which seemed terribly innocent.

"Sounds like something I'd enjoy,"—Jed said, smiling—"once I get settled in."

"We're not going to give him much time for riding," Roger interrupted. "Not until after soccer season, anyway. The coach already has him singled out as first-string forward."

"We're glad you're on the team," Caitlin said. "With Roger as captain, we're going to have a great season." Caitlin glanced at Roger, who seemed flattered by her praise. Then through slightly lowered lashes, she looked directly back at Jed. "But I know it will be even better now."

Jed only smiled. "Hope I can live up to that."

Roger turned to Jed. "We've got to go."

"Fine." Jed nodded.

Caitlin noticed Dorothy, who had been silent during Jed and Caitlin's conversation. She was now staring at Jed wistfully as he and Roger headed toward the door.

Caitlin quickly leaned over to whisper, "Dorothy, did you notice the way Roger was looking at you?"

Her attention instantly diverted, Dorothy looked away from Jed to look at Caitlin. "Me?" She sounded surprised.

"Yeah. He really seems interested."

"Oh, I don't think so." Despite her attraction to Jed, Dorothy seemed flattered. "He's hardly ever looked at me before."

"You were standing behind me and probably couldn't notice, but take my word for it."

Dorothy glanced at the star soccer player's retreating back. Her expression was doubtful, but for the moment she'd forgotten her pursuit of Jed, and Caitlin took that opportunity to focus her own attention on the new boy from Montana. She knew she only had a moment more to make that unforgettable impression on him before the two boys were gone. Quickly she walked forward. Her voice was light but loud enough to carry to the girls behind her.

"We were just going in your direction, anyway," she called. "Why don't we walk along just to show you what strong supporters of the team we are?"

Looking surprised, Roger said, "That's fine by us. Right, Jed?"

"Whatever you say."

Caitlin thought he sounded pleased by the attention. Quickly, before the other girls joined them, she stepped between the two boys. Roger immediately tried to pull her hand close to his side. She wanted to swat him off, but instead, gave his hand a squeeze, then let go. She was pleased when Diana fell in step beside Roger. Turning to Jed, Caitlin smiled and said, "There must be a thousand questions you still have about the school and the area. Have you been to Virginia before?"

"A few times. I've seen a little of the countryside."

"And you like it?"

As they walked out the door of the building, Jed turned his head so that he could look down into her upturned face and nodded. There was a bright twinkle in his eyes.

Caitlin took that twinkle as encouragement, and her own eyes grew brighter. "So much goes on around here at this time of year. Has anyone told you about the fall dance this weekend?"

"I think Matt Jenks did. I'm rooming with him."

"It'll be great—a real good band," Caitlin cooed. In the background she heard the sound of the others' voices, but they didn't matter. Jed Michaels was listening to *her*.

They walked together for only another minute, down the brick footpath that connected the classroom buildings to the rest of the elegant campus. Caitlin told him all she could about the upcoming dance, stopping short of asking him to be her date. She wasn't going to throw herself at him. She wouldn't have to, anyway. She knew it would be only a matter of time before he would be hers.

It didn't take them long to reach the turnoff for the soccer field. "I guess this is where I get off," she said lightly. "See you around."

"See you soon," he answered and left.

Caitlin smiled to herself. This handsome boy from Montana wasn't going to be an easy mark, but this was an adequate beginning. She wanted him—and what Caitlin wanted, Caitlin got.

"You going back to the dorm, Caitlin?" Morgan asked.

"Yeah, I've got a ton of reading to do for English lit." Caitlin spoke easily, but her thoughts were on the smile Jed Michaels had given her just before he'd left.

"Somerson really piled it on tonight, didn't she?" Gloria Parks muttered.

"Who cares about homework," Caitlin replied. "I want to hear what you guys think of Jed."

"Not bad at all." Tenny giggled.

"We ought to be asking *you*, Caitlin," Morgan added. "You got all his attention."

Caitlin brought her thoughts back to the present and laughed. "Did I? I hadn't even noticed," she said coyly.

"At least Roger's got some competition now," Jessica Stark, a usually quiet redhead, remarked. "He was really getting *unbearable*."

"There's probably a lot more to Roger than meets the eye," Dorothy said in his defense.

"I agree. Roger's not bad. And what do you expect," Caitlin added, "when all he hears is how he's the school star."

The girls started crossing the lawns from the grouping of Highgate classroom buildings toward the dorms. The magnificent grounds of the exclusive boarding school were spread out around them. The ivy-covered walls of the original school building had changed little in the two hundred years since it had been constructed as the manor house for a prosperous plantation. A sweeping carpet of lawn had replaced the tilled fields of the past; and the smaller buildings had been converted into dormitories and staff quarters. The horse stable had been expanded, and several structures had been added—classroom buildings, a gymnasium complete with an indoor pool, tennis and racketball courts—but the architecture of the new buildings blended in well with that of the old.

"Caitlin, isn't that your grandmother's car in the visitors' parking lot?" Morgan pointed toward the graveled parking area off the oak-shaded main drive. A sleek, silver Mercedes sports coupe was gleaming in the sunlight there.

"So it is." Caitlin frowned momentarily. "Wonder what she's doing here? I must have left something at the house last time I was home for the weekend."

"My dream car!" Gloria exclaimed, holding one hand up to adjust her glasses. "I've told Daddy he absolutely *must* buy me one for my sixteenth birthday."

"And what did he say?" Jessica asked.

Gloria made a face. "That I had to settle for his three-year-old Datsun or get a bicycle."

"Beats walking," Morgan said, reaching into her bag for another candy bar.

"But I'm dying to have a car like your grandmother's."

"It's not bad." Caitlin glanced up at the car. "She has the Bentley, too, but this is the car she uses when she wants to drive herself instead of being chauffeured."

"Think she'll let you bring it here for your senior year?"

Caitlin shrugged and mimicked her grandmother's cultured tones. "'It's not wise to spoil one.' Besides, I've always preferred Jaguars."

Caitlin paused on the brick path, and the other girls stopped beside her. "You know, I really should go say hello to my grandmother. She's probably waiting for me." She turned quickly to the others. "We've got to have a meeting for this fundraiser. How about tonight—my room, at seven?"

"Sure."

"Great."

"Darn, I've got to study for an exam tomorrow," Jessica grumbled, "but let me know what you decide."

"Me, too," Kim commented. "I was on the courts all afternoon yesterday practicing for Sunday's tennis tournament and really got behind with my studying."

"Okay, we'll fill you guys in, but make sure you come to the next meeting. And I don't want any excuses. If you miss the meeting, you're out!" Caitlin stressed firmly. "I'll catch the rest of you later, then."

All the girls walked away except Dorothy, who lingered behind. Just then, a tall, elegantly dressed, silver-haired woman walked briskly down the stairs from the administrative office in the main school building. She moved directly toward the Mercedes, quickly opened the driver's door, and slid in behind the wheel.

Caitlin's arm shot up in greeting, but Regina Ryan

never glanced her way. Instead, she started the engine and immediately swung out of the parking area and down the curving drive.

For an instant Caitlin stopped in her tracks. Then with a wide, carefree smile, she turned back to Dorothy and laughed. "I just remembered. She called last night and said she was dropping off my allowance money but would be in a hurry and couldn't stay. My memory really *is* bad. I'll run over and pick it up now."

As Caitlin turned, Dorothy lightly grabbed Caitlin's elbow and spoke softly. "I know you're in a hurry, but can I talk to you for a second, Caitlin? Did you mean what you said about Roger? Was he really looking at me?"

"I told you he was," Caitlin said impatiently, anxious to get Dorothy out of the picture. "Would I lie to you?"

"Oh, no. It's just that when I went over to talk to him, he didn't seem that interested. He was more interested in listening to what you and Jed were saying."

"Roger's just nosy."

"Well, I wondered. You know, I haven't had any dates since I transferred—"

"Dorothy! You're worried about dates? Are you crazy?" Caitlin grinned broadly. "And as far as Roger goes, wait and see. Believe me." She gave a breezy wave. "I've got to go."

"Yeah, okay. And, thanks, Caitlin."

"Anytime."

Without a backward glance, Caitlin walked quickly to the administration office. The story about her allowance had been a fabrication. Regina Ryan had given Caitlin more than enough spending money when she'd been home two weeks earlier, but it would be all over campus in a minute if the girls thought there was anything marring Caitlin's seemingly perfect life.

Running up the steps and across the main marble-floored lobby that had once been the elegant entrance hall of the plantation house, she walked quickly into the dean's office and smiled warmly at Mrs. Forbes, the dean's secretary.

"Hi, Mrs. Forbes."

"Hello, Caitlin. Can I help you?"

"I came to pick up the message my grandmother just left."

"Message?" Mrs. Forbes frowned.

"Yes." Caitlin continued to look cheerful. "I just saw her leaving and figured she was in a hurry and left a message for me here."

"No, she just met on some school board business briefly with Dean Fleming."

"She didn't leave anything for me?"

"I can check with the part-time girl if you like."

"Thanks." Caitlin's smile had faded, but she waited as Mrs. Forbes stepped into a small room at the rear.

She returned in a second, shaking her head. "Sorry, Caitlin."

Caitlin forced herself to smile. "No problem, Mrs. Forbes. It wasn't important, anyway. She'll probably be on the phone with me ten times tonight."

As Caitlin hurried from the main building and set out again toward the dorm, her beautiful face was grim. Why was she always trying to fool herself? She knew there was no chance her grandmother would call just to say hello. But nobody would ever know that: She would make certain of it. Not Mrs. Forbes, or any of the kids; not even her roommate, Ginny. Not anyone!

Like it so far? Want to read more? LOVING will be available in May 1985.* It will be on sale wherever Bantam paperbacks are sold. The other two books in the trilogy, LOVE DENIED and TRUE LOVE, will also be published in 1985.

*Outside the United States and Canada, books will be available approximately three months later. Check with your local bookseller for further details.

You'll fall in love with all the Sweet Dream romances. Reading these stories, you'll be reminded of yourself or of someone you know. There's Jennie, the *California Girl*, who becomes an outsider when her family moves to Texas. And Cindy, the *Little Sister*, who's afraid that Christine, the oldest in the family, will steal her new boyfriend. Don't miss any of the Sweet Dreams romances.

☐ 24292	IT MUST BE MAGIC #26		$2.25
	Marian Woodruff		
☐ 22681	TOO YOUNG FOR LOVE #27		$1.95
	Gailanne Maravel		
☐ 23053	TRUSTING HEARTS #28		$1.95
	Jocelyn Saal		
☐ 24312	NEVER LOVE A COWBOY #29		$2.25
	Jesse Dukore		
☐ 24293	LITTLE WHITE LIES #30		$2.25
	Lois I. Fisher		
☐ 23189	TOO CLOSE FOR COMFORT #31		$1.95
	Debra Spector		
☐ 24837	DAY DREAMER #32		$2.25
	Janet Quin-Harkin		
☐ 23283	DEAR AMANDA #33		$1.95
	Rosemary Vernon		
☐ 23287	COUNTRY GIRL #34		$1.95
	Melinda Pollowitz		
☐ 24336	FORBIDDEN LOVE #35		$2.25
	Marian Woodruff		
☐ 24338	SUMMER DREAMS #36		$2.25
	Barbara Conklin		
☐ 23340	PORTRAIT OF LOVE #37		$1.95
	Jeanette Noble		
☐ 24331	RUNNING MATES #38		$2.25
	Jocelyn Saal		
☐ 24340	FIRST LOVE #39		$2.25
	Debra Spector		
☐ 24315	SECRETS #40		$2.25
	Anna Aaron		
☐ 24838	THE TRUTH ABOUT ME AND BOBBY V. #41		$2.25
	Janetta Johns		
☐ 23532	THE PERFECT MATCH #42		$1.95
	Marian Woodruff		
☐ 23533	TENDER-LOVING-CARE #43		$1.95
	Anne Park		
☐ 23534	LONG DISTANCE LOVE #44		$1.95
	Jesse Dukore		
☐ 24341	DREAM PROM #45		$2.25
	Margaret Burman		
☐ 23697	ON THIN ICE #46		$1.95
	Jocelyn Saal		
☐ 23743	TE AMO MEANS I LOVE YOU #47		$1.95
	Deborah Kent		
☐ 24688	SECRET ADMIRER #81		$2.25
	Debra Spector		
☐ 24383	HEY, GOOD LOOKING #82		$2.25
	Jane Polcovar		

Prices and availability subject to change without notice.

Bantam Books, Inc., Dept. SD, 414 East Golf Road, Des Plaines, Ill. 60016

Please send me the books I have checked above. I am enclosing $_____
(please add $1.25 to cover postage and handling). Send check or money order
—no cash or C.O.D.'s please.

Mr/Mrs/Miss_____

Address_____

City_____State/Zip_____

SD—3/85

Please allow four to six weeks for delivery. This offer expires 9/85.

SPECIAL MONEY SAVING OFFER

Now you can have an up-to-date listing of Bantam's hundreds of titles plus take advantage of our unique and exciting bonus book offer. A special offer which gives you the opportunity to purchase a Bantam book for only 50¢. Here's how!

By ordering any five books at the regular price per order, you can also choose any other single book listed (up to a $4.95 value) for just 50¢. Some restrictions do apply, but for further details why not send for Bantam's listing of titles today!

Just send us your name and address plus 50¢ to defray the postage and handling costs.

BANTAM BOOKS, INC.
Dept. FC, 414 East Golf Road, Des Plaines, Ill 60016

Mr./Mrs./Miss/Ms. _____
                            (please print)

Address _____

City_____ State_____ Zip_____

FC—3/84